kith

kith

p.h. newby

Little, Brown   Boston–Toronto

Second Printing

LIBRARY OF CONGRESS CATALOGING IN PUBLICATION DATA

Newby, Percy Howard, 1918-
  Kith.

  I. Title.
PZ3.N4294Ki3 [PR6027.E855] 823'.9'14 77-5204
ISBN 0-316-60420-8

For Huw

chapteR 1

 When you consider what Nadia eventually became it is extraordinary anyone ever thought she had once tried to throw herself off the Great Pyramid. She was a practical woman and would have foreseen the difficulties. It is like a builder's yard up there. The structure is eroded and goes down in clumsy great steps, so it is impossible to hurl yourself from the highest point in the hope of landing in the sand at the foot, or indeed any significant distance down the side. Even if you kept going, you would just bounce from one stone block to the next.

True, tourists are kept off the top nowadays because people have had fatal falls; but they didn't fall right to the bottom and nothing less would have satisfied Nadia, certainly not the young Nadia I knew, probably not the princess she became; assuming, that is, she wanted to jump and didn't just slip. This was a long time ago. You could climb up, day or night, without much supervision then. But it was always dangerous.

Writing about her is the only way to possess her. No one did really, certainly not Uncle Raymond, or me, or all those others. She was her own woman. Writing about her creates a sense of her presence. I can even see her, in a manner of speaking. As I write I feel I understand her. Not otherwise. When I stop I lose her.

I wear the old kit for writing, usually the khaki shorts with flaps you can let down and button below the knees as a protection against mosquitoes. I also have a pair with the flaps cut off. There wasn't much malaria in the desert. I have bush shirts, issue boots

1

and puttees, winter-weight battledress, a glengary, regimental badges and division flashes, a flat Guardsman's cap with a steep peak, stripes, pips, crowns, greatcoat, steel helmet, gas mask and gas cape. I never had that camouflaged battledress; they didn't issue it in the desert or Western Europe, at least, not to the lot I was with. My appearance as I sit writing is not what you'd expect from seeing me at the Features Desk.

The assumption has worn thin that there can be some final taking stock of what happens in the world. It can just be discerned through the iridescence of despair, nothing to do with any vestigial belief in a Last Judgement or absolutes of any kind. Perhaps it persists because of what happens in the schools. In the museum of academic opinion there is the semblance of a verdict – hesitating, provisional, sceptical. And yet somewhere, at some time, we obscurely feel, there will be more than this. There will be a real confirmation or denial. Justice is too difficult a word to use lightly. So, we don't use it, not while we are waiting.

In March, 1941, I was one of the rearguard on a troopcarrier in Suez Roads which, contrary to what one might expect of this arm of the Red Sea, was fogbound. The fog smelled strongly of petrol and what I later learned to be goat. We had just made the three month voyage round the Cape from the U.K. The rest of my unit, the 2nd 33rd Australian Infantry Battalion, had gone ashore in lighters and I was with half a dozen other men keeping an eye on the equipment and stores until they too could be put ashore. We were playing cards on a hatch cover when Uncle Raymond, whom I had not seen for a couple of years, suddenly appeared out of the fog, dressed as a British Army captain.

"There you are, then, Tishy," he said in his flat, robot voice. "Your officer said I'd find you. You realise the Biblical significance of this fog? Egyptian darkness. Though it could have been a sandstorm. Pity you can't see the view. Over there is Sinai. Behind you is the Egyptian desert. St. Antony's monastery is down there. In happier times I would have taken you to these places."

2

"Tishy?" said one of the Aussies.

"There was a racehorse called that," I said. "Had a way of standing with his front legs crossed."

"My nephew was born with his legs crossed," Uncle Raymond explained.

I said, "I wouldn't be the first of you to call me by that name."

Having been a non-combatant stretcher-bearer through that French rout and not being allowed to carry arms I was more aggressive than these Australian infantrymen. It was my ambition to get out of the Medical Corps into a combat unit where you had something to protect yourself with. It wasn't my nature to be passive. On the slog out of Belgium and on the pier at Calais I had been useless with panic.

I had still not recovered from the surprise of seeing Uncle Raymond, and, what is more, seeing him dressed up as an officer. I knew he was in Egypt and I had vaguely expected to bump into him some time or other before going on to Greece with these Aussies. But he was a teacher, a civilian. He had been out in Egypt teaching since the early Thirties. I had thought of him giving me a meal in his flat in Cairo. It simply hadn't entered my mind he'd come and welcome me to this part of the war. He looked quite natty in his Sam Browne. He was wearing a great holster with the butt of a pistol sticking out of it, rather in the manner of the Canadian Mounties. Once we had moved off to another part of the deck he began asking me about the family and how they were standing up to the bombing.

"What is to become of us all, Tishy?"

He was a big, fresh-faced, bony man with a turnip grin that he would maintain for minutes on end even when you were telling him something unpleasant. His ears were curiously small and white. He stooped, grinning and swinging his head from side to side, his feet planted wide apart. "This fog makes my eyes run. It's the fumes from the refinery. Do you think the Germans will get to the Delta? I trust you've brought some good equipment with you. You need very heavy, fast tanks, ones that don't sink into the sand. Do you think the War Office have thought of that,

Tishy? It worries me terribly they may have forgotten it's all desert here."

He was my mother's brother and I thought of him as rather a brittle, very reserved, intense sort of man. It bothered me that he was not brittle and reserved at that moment and I even supposed it was because he was scared and wanted me to reassure him by producing some marvellous secret weapon. He was not a coward. Far from it, as I later learned. He would, oddly enough, have made a good professional soldier. But in that Suez fog he seemed to be wobbling. His anxiety was probably caused by the sight of my face and the way it reminded him of his sister and the rest of the family back home.

"I'm worried about your aunt," he said just as he was about to go ashore, by way of a footnote to everything we had been saying about the war, the family, the fog and so on. That was how he introduced the subject. But I immediately knew that so far as Uncle Raymond was concerned the real issue had at last been touched on. This was what life meant. This was why he had asked some pal in a key position certain questions about troop movements he had no business to be asking and, on learning the unit to which he happened to know I was attached had come into Port Tewfik on the *Franconia*, had thumbed a lift down. He was by nature a family man. Talking to me was the nearest thing to a family council he could arrange.

"Which one?" I said, because Mother and he had a sister living in California; and there was Aunt Gwyneth, Dad's sister, who ran a sweet-shop in Ironbridge.

"My wife, your Aunt Nadia," he said. "She's technically a British subject but she's still got Egyptian nationality too. I've told her to burn her British papers if the Germans get in. That's not what I'm worried about."

I hated to tell him but this was the first I had heard of Aunt Nadia and he said, oh yes, they'd got married in the spring of the previous year (later, we worked out it was the very day I helped to set up No. 8 Casualty Clearing Station on Calais pier) and now there was Trouble. Nothing to do with the war. If Hitler had never existed there would have been this Trouble. Be-

4

ing nineteen years old at the time I found this hard to believe; I still thought the cause of trouble was Other People. I didn't believe in the Devil, exactly. But Bad Things, it seemed to me, except those to do with health or lack of money, were brought about by Wicked Individuals out there; I wasn't too sure they weren't responsible for bad health and bankruptcy, too. I still had some belief in witchcraft. That was another way of putting it. Hitler was the Great Witch of the moment. During his ascendancy no other witchcraft had power. So I was sceptical about Aunt Nadia's trouble existing independently of Hitler. *Pace* Uncle Raymond, it had everything to do with the war.

I was not well-informed about his marital affairs. There had been a Great Scandal before the war but I was still at school and not privy to information of that sort. It was, I gathered, all just Too Shocking for my young ears. Then I was caught up in this war, and training, and going over to France and into Belgium. What with one thing and another Uncle Raymond dropped low in my list of interests; to be honest, he was still sufficiently low in March, 1941, for me to be annoyed he should want to talk about himself at all. I was the one who had had a tough time. I was the one booked for Greece where, no doubt, my ambulance would immediately be dive-bombed. In those days we all knew nothing maddened Jerry so much as a Red Cross. Even though Uncle Raymond had not mentioned his domestic troubles until last I was none the less disgusted.

"'Bye, then," I said as I saw him down the ladder to where he had a launch waiting.

"You're going up to Base Camp at Qassassin," said Uncle Raymond, "but I don't think it right you should be serving with the Australians. I shall see what can be done about that. I have a certain influence at H.Q. We'll be in touch. I just wanted you to see a friendly face on your arrival, so as you wouldn't feel too far from home. Didn't mean to afflict you with my private troubles. It just popped out. Forgive me, Tishy." Once more, the turnip grin and a braying, irrelevant, donkey laugh that set up echoes in the fog as he went clattering down the steps to a launch that was afloat on a sea of cigarette cartons, empty beer

5

bottles, cabbage leaves and other kitchen refuse that could just be detected through the murk.

If I had gone to Greece with the Aussies I should have been back in much the same Stuka bombed hell as I'd recently left behind me in France. It turned out worse than I'd feared because the 2nd 33rd Battalion never got as far as Greece. The Germans were already in Athens. So the Aussies went to Crete and none of the medicos came back from there, not until after the war; and most of the Aussies did not come back even then. It all turned out worse than I'd expected but what I did expect was sufficiently bad to make me think of deserting. We were all kitted up at some camp just outside Alexandria ready to embark for Crete when an N.C.O. came round the tents – it was about two in the morning, just when everyone was expecting the signal to move off – shouting my name. I went out to meet him.

He said, "You Private Cozens? Your uncle's dying. That's your uncle, isn't it, C'p'n Foulkes? There's a travel warrant at the company office."

It all turned out to be a mistake. Certainly Uncle Raymond had been ill. Sandfly fever developed into pneumonia and for several days he was on the Dangerously Ill list but when I caught up with him he was convalescent with a bottle of champagne in an ice box. Apparently it was quite true he had the ear of somebody in Cairo. To him he made this point about a British soldier attached to an Australian infantry battalion – I could explain why *that* came about – and at roughly the time he was stricken my posting to the staff of No. 6 General Hospital came through. There was the usual military misunderstanding over all this. My posting order and Uncle Raymond's medical documents ended up in the same folder. So we both went to No. 6 even though Uncle Raymond, according to the rules then prevailing, should really have gone to Ismailia with all the other Canal Defence Force casualties. Pleased as I was to miss the Crete boat I was not at all pleased to be carrying bed pans in a vast tented hospital in the desert when I really wanted to get hold of something aggressive, a rifle at least. By then I knew that what I really wanted was to get into the Artillery and shoot off one of those Bofors at the Luftwaffe.

So I found myself, off duty, dropping in to see Uncle Raymond. Being a Seriously Ill officer, he had his section of the tent partitioned off and there was no one to overhear. He had not been allowed to start on the champagne and it had merely been parked in his ice box as an inducement to get well. He must have been one of the first men in the Middle East to be given penicillin. Once he had finished his course of the stuff and been able to sit up, better still walk about a bit, the Q.A. Ward Sister had promised him a glass of champagne. But until that time arrived he was not supposed to stir a finger; shaving was out of the question so he had grown quite a beard, the exact colour of the sand outside.

"Tishy, you've got to go to Cairo for me." He was not supposed even to move his head and his voice was not much above a whisper. "You've got to see Nadia."

Other chaps had been able to get away to Cairo on week-end passes in spite of the flap but at that time I was not allowed even to leave the camp. I had button-holed the Company Officer about getting a transfer to a combat unit and the R.S.M. put me on a charge the moment he heard of it because he thought I was angling to get back to the U.K. for infantry training. The R.S.M. in truth occupied my thoughts more than Uncle Raymond did. I explained about being confined to the camp for another two weeks but Uncle Raymond said he would talk to the M.O. in charge of his case. Recovery was out of the question until he had news of his wife; even his sanity might be affected.

"You must tell her nothing about my past though." He tried to lift his head off the pillow, couldn't quite manage it and tried to see me by swivelling his eyes. They showed a lot of white and what with his beard and hoarse whisper he looked alarming.

"No, I won't tell her anything about your past," I said. The next of kin of anybody on the D.I. list was automatically informed. We were only about forty miles from Cairo. Aunt Nadia could have been at the hospital within a couple of hours. Either she did not know or she did not want to know.

"You've got to go today. You've got to go now. I can't stand it, Tishy." He was drawing in his breath in an ugly, laughing way which might have been sobbing. If the Q.A. came in and saw him distressed like this there would be hell to pay and, of course, this is precisely what happened. Sister Somebody-or-Other came in and I stood up because she was an officer and I was a private.

"What's this then? Stop that row! You're not dying, Captain Foulkes, so you can stop upsetting everybody."

Not being on duty I was sent back to my quarters but a couple of hours later I was told to parade at the Company Office where Captain Springer looked me over from behind his desk and said, "You're to go to Cairo tomorrow, Cozens, on special leave. There's a truck leaving at half past seven. Now you can go off and see your uncle and try to calm him down a bit, for God's sake!"

By this time it was dark and Uncle Raymond's ward was illuminated by a hurricane lamp. Major Gee, the Registrar, was standing with the *Egyptian Gazette* held up to this lamp, reading aloud, no doubt for my uncle's benefit, an account of the sinking of a German convoy in the Med. When he saw me he said, "Ah, Cozens, we thought it would be an idea if you called on your aunt. Obviously there's a misunderstanding. We've been on to Cairo. They've been delivering the usual bumph and doing it by hand. But she won't answer the door and chaps just have to leave it in her letter box in the hall. They know she's there because the porter says so. So we thought maybe she'd open the door for you. One of the family."

Uncle Raymond had plainly been given a shot of something to calm him down and the remarks made by Major Gee had the same analgesic intent. He lay there, not seeming to breathe, with his bearded chin stuck out, just shining – white brow and temple, sunken cheeks, straight nose and tufted chin – all shining with sweat. When Major Gee had gone, Uncle Raymond began working his lips to produce a sound and at last brought out the words, "My wallet is in that basket. You'll find money and if you can't remember the address it is 5, Midan Ismailia, Flat Number 3. You'll find papers in there with the address on if you forget it. When you see your aunt tell her all I want to know is how she is. You understand that? No other questions. If she is in good health and is happy that is all I want to know. Tell her I've been ill. But remember! Be discreet. Don't talk about the family. Nothing about my past."

"What's wrong about that?"

"I forbid you to talk about the past."

"All right. I'll keep off it," I said. "The way she's behaving I'll be lucky even to get a sight of her."

"Swear you won't talk about the past."

In the eyes of the family Uncle Raymond and I had a lot in common. He was the first of the Foulkeses to earn his living without taking his tie off and when I, too, first stayed on at school and then said I was going to college the Cozenses realised they had another non-worker on their hands. They were not censorious. They might have conceded, if challenged, it was possible to work with your head as well as with your hands but in their hearts they would have known differently. Work had to be physical.

Grandad Foulkes was a greengrocer and he shod horses on the side because there was already a shortage of blacksmiths in those days. He used to be up at three every morning to drive the old Morris truck up to Brentford Market for fruit and vegetables. He ran the store until midday, Granny sitting at the cash desk. In the afternoon she took over completely, helped by my mother as soon as she was old enough, while Grandad went round to the forge and shod tradesmen's cobs, farm horses, riding-school ponies, not as a real blacksmith would, with shoes made from cold bars but with mass-produced shoes from Birmingham he just heated up and hammered to the precise size.

He was the first man in our parts to use this technique. It was not well viewed. But what with the greengrocery business, the shoe-ing and the pig-breeding which came to play an increasingly important part in his life – the daily swill cooking, the mucking out of the sties, the buying and the selling, the slaughtering during a swine fever epidemic, the straightforward slaughtering for pig-meat (Grandad used to do it himself, there was no need for a licence in those days, and I've helped him hoist a pig on a pulley and stick him in the throat) – this was all hard, sweating, graft and Uncle Raymond played no part in

9

it because he was good at books and won a scholarship to Reading University. The scandal that hit him in the early Thirties had something to do with the fancy schoolmastering life he was leading. This was never actually said but you had the feeling that if only he'd worked in the business he would never have been disgraced. Then I let it be known I wasn't going to work either. I too was going to read books all day.

If anything, my old man worked even harder than Grandad because he had a sort of farm, he did a certain amount of building and decorating, he had a couple of taxis on which he did all the running repairs himself, and then there was the undertaking. He branched out into undertaking after buying a second-hand hearse cheap. He was only a part-time undertaker. He liked to oblige in the busy seasons which always seemed to be just before Christmas and again in the late spring; or perhaps it was when farm work was slack. He was a terrible farmer. He was terrible at everything really and he exhausted himself at it. He was always patching up the barn just after the rain storm that soaked the hay. Crops were sown just that bit too late. Roots rotted in the clamp, the hedging and ditching usually seemed to be done after dark by the light of hurricane lamps, and yet he could be away on some building or decorating job the very time he ought to have been using fine weather in the fields. I can see now there was deliberation in this lack of method. It ensured he worked harder, and mother worked too; what with the housework and the chickens and the books for the undertaking and the books for the taxis, they worked Sundays and Bank Holidays, they worked as though they wanted to stupefy themselves. If ever they thought about mother's brother, Raymond, as they might on Christmas Day, it was as a man who had dodged the real business of life, good luck to him, and the scandal was all part of the book reading and not working. Everybody but Uncle Raymond and I worked physically very hard, and by choice not necessity because they were not interested in money and indeed were careless with it.

At the time I thought the family were stupid and felt a bit sorry for them. They conditioned my thinking about Uncle Raymond, though, even though like him I wasn't going to do any work either. What it amounted to, as I sat listening to him in G Ward, Officers' Annexe, No. 6 General Hospital, was a prejudice that his troubles were not to be taken too seriously. With my upbringing you wouldn't have taken Hamlet's troubles all that seriously. They ate and drank well in Elsinore and nobody did a stroke of work.

"Tishy," Uncle Raymond was saying, "Come closer! Put your head down! It isn't necessary you should actually talk to her. I mean, if you talk to her so much the better. But if there is any difficulty I shall be perfectly content if you can tell me you've seen her, and she's quite well and looks happy."

"Does she talk English? I don't know any Egyptian."

"It isn't Egyptian, it's Arabic. There's no Egyptian language. I mean, there is but it isn't spoken any more. There's an old priest in your Aunt Nadia's family who reads liturgical Coptic, you see, but I don't think he understands it. You know what Coptic is, don't you, Tishy? Your Aunt is a Copt. She's Christian though a Monophysite which, as you know, is the belief there is only One Nature in the Person of Jesus Christ and not Two as the rest of us have it." I could hear those capital letters.

"Is she black?" There is no exaggerating my ignorance at this time. Uncle Raymond was talking so quietly, not much above a whisper, I had to hold my head very close to his. His breath stank and the effect in that dark tent (the lamp had been doused because of an air-raid warning) was to make me think of tombs, the mouldering dead, mummies and animal-headed monsters. This was the world in which my imagination placed Aunt Nadia. How would I communicate with an elderly Egyptian lady whose language was not a spoken one even if I got so far as making the attempt? How would I even know her when I saw her?

"Black, Tishy? She's whiter than we are because Coptic women of that class never go out in the sun. She'll speak English to you. If you should get to talking and she asks you whether it is true my first marriage ended in divorce you have only to tell the truth. You know what that is, don't you?"

"No."

"You don't remember your Aunt Treasure?"

This was an extraordinary name for a woman and I had to say yes, I'd heard the name before but I didn't realise she'd been Uncle Raymond's first wife and I certainly didn't remember meeting her.

"But we took you out in a punt once when you were quite a tiny boy. Don't you remember the elvers?"

"No."

"There was a chain going down into the water and when we pulled it up there was a wooden box full of baby eels. We took the lid off for you to see."

No, I couldn't remember and I could not understand why he was so anxious for me to remember. Not long before he had been forbidding me to talk to Aunt Nadia about the past. Uncle Raymond's disappointment with me was so great he seemed quite demoralised by it.

"Perhaps you'd better not go," he said after a long pause. "There might be a letter from her in the morning."

"Of course," I said, trying to cheer him up, "I knew there was some scandal."

"What do you mean?"

"I didn't know what it was exactly but I knew there'd been something awful."

To my surprise he began laughing in a tinny sort of way. "Yes, it was awful. Your aunt left me and went to live with a Post Office engineer. He was responsible for the maintenance of poles and wires and those little china cups you see on the horizontal arms or slats at the top of the poles."

"Insulators."

"That's right. His responsibilities extended over a wide area in the West Midlands. So naturally there was a divorce," he said, rather as though there wouldn't have been if the chap's responsibilities had been in some other part of the country.

"Where were you teaching then?" If he said Worcestershire or Herefordshire or, anyway, somewhere west of Banbury the point would have been cleared up but he said no, he was already teaching in Egypt at the time, at Beni Suef actually, and Treasure really liked the life so you couldn't put the break down to that. She just preferred somebody else to him. That was the harsh truth. He would never have admitted it in words if he hadn't been weakened by illness. He really had thought he was dying. Oh why, for God's sake why, hadn't Nadia got in touch with him? If he hadn't treated her with absolute candour (he admitted he hadn't) there was no justification for neglecting him in his extremity. He was her legal husband. There really had been a divorce and it was absurd to say Treasure was still his wife.

"Who says that?"

"Nadia does."

"You mean because her religion doesn't recognise divorce?"

"Oh no, Copts marry and divorce and remarry. She just thinks I've got a wife in England and she's just a concubine."

"But when you married Aunt Nadia I suppose she knew about your first marriage?"

"No," said Uncle Raymond shortly.

"Why not?"

"I didn't tell her."

"And she found out?"

"Yes." He was almost inaudible.

I didn't know what to say to this except I supposed documents had needed producing, or at least statements required, that would have brought the truth into the open. He said no, he'd been afraid of a difficulty of that sort but there was only one form on which he had needed to tell a direct lie and in the circumstances he thought it was worth it.

"I don't see why you didn't tell her."

"It would have been undignified. Your Aunt Treasure preferred another man to me and it was all very humiliating. Figuratively speaking, I was abandoned at the dark roadside while she drove off with her *inamorato*, lights blazing. How could I possibly retail something so disgusting to an innocent girl like your Aunt Nadia? She would have despised me. I've changed my mind. I don't want you to go and see her after all. There'll be a letter in the morning. If there isn't I shall be up and about myself in a few days and I can go myself. I feel better after our little chat, Tishy."

But I went to Cairo on that 7.30 truck nonetheless because my main reason for going all along had not been to look up Aunt Nadia but to see the Chief Clerk in the office of O.C. Troops, Egypt. I'd known this man as Sergeant-Clerk in the Hussars with gunshot wounds to his right thigh and abdomen. He was in my C.C.S. on Calais pier. We came out of Calais on the same paddle steamer and I thought well of him at the time because he gave a cod commentary on the evacuation which had us all laughing a bit hysterically. It was sheer chance I found he was in H.Q. I was doing duty in the hospital office one night (a lot of clerks had just been posted and I was standing in) when the phone rang and there was this unforgettable nasal voice. I didn't recognise it immediately but I had to take down a message he was dictating and I asked him to authenticate it by giving his name, rank and number. Razier, he said. It was a name you remembered, so we identified each other, and he told me he had an office job at Base now because of his leg and he'd be really glad to see me when I had leave. The point was that if my own unit were blocking the possibility of a transfer Razier might be able to pull a few strings in H.Q. and get me into a combat unit.

The war was being lost, Crete had been taken by German and Italian parachutists led, so rumour had it, by Primo Carnera, ex-heavyweight boxing champion of the world. Yet Uncle Raymond still thought it possible for me to take an interest in his marital affairs. To me they seemed plain trivial. My concern was what happened when the Axis forces moved into the Delta. By that time I wanted to have a weapon in my hands and if there was no regular way of getting a transfer I even had thoughts of deserting, so that I could join up again with false papers and this time into the mob of my choice, the Armoured Corps or Artillery. There were stories of men facing court martial for serious crime who had deserted and joined up again as being the safest way of

14

covering their tracks. In Cairo you could buy whatever papers you wanted. Some men, it was said, just deserted and lived with the Bedouin, taking a wife and really going native to get out of the war. I told Razier I'd desert altogether rather than go through another blitz as a non-combatant.

Razier was his old merry self. He was a little dark man with a mouth like a pike. More even than Uncle Raymond he had that trick of grinning all the time, even when there was nothing to grin about. We sat in his office drinking sweet tea and he made quips I didn't respond to until he got exasperated and said, "They'd pick you up but that's neither here nor there. You wouldn't really want to desert. That's as much as to say you don't give a damn who wins."

"Sometimes I feel like that."

"What about Hitler?"

"You'd have to be bloody evil to believe the stories you hear about Hitler and I'm not evil, I'm ordinary."

"I can't help you, son."

I was so cross I came straight out of the Semiramis Hotel, which was where H.Q. was on the right bank of the Nile with a view straight over to the Pyramids, and walked back into the town with the idea of finding some bar or café where I might make a contact. I still had Uncle Raymond's wallet in my pocket and I knew it contained over a hundred Egyptian pounds which was more than enough to – well, do what? I had my back to the river and was walking into an open space where trams seemed to converge from different parts of the city.

I saw the name of this place on a smart building of eight or nine floors, Midan Ismailia, and next to it a dark, crumbling three-storey building with iron verandahs, shuttered upstairs windows and leprous stucco panels of flowers and fruit between them. Number 5. The figure was up there in European as well as Arab numbers. Uncle Raymond's home. Even now Aunt Nadia might be concealed behind the shutters and I thought I would go in on the off chance, not so much on Uncle Raymond's behalf, but because it occurred to me that Aunt Nadia, being

Egyptian, might have some suggestion for concealing me in the city, or getting me away to the south, to the Sudan. She might have relatives in a remote village.

In fact, it was not at all difficult to find Aunt Nadia. Flat Number 3 was on the first floor. I walked up the stone stairs (there was no lift) and rang the bell in a door with a glass and ironwork top only to find it opened almost immediately by a girl of about my own age. She was wearing a yellow silk dress with sleeves that came down to just below her elbows. On the fingers of both hands she had rings with bulky stones in them and I looked at these as a way of avoiding her face and eyes because they moved me so much I was embarrassed. She was impossibly, absurdly beautiful. I had never seen anyone to touch her, nor ever have. She was fragrant, edible, even – to my startled eyes – luminous.

"Does Mrs Foulkes live here?" I asked.

"Yes." A low, almost chuckling kind of voice. It threw the final switch and involuntarily the flesh responded. I too could step out of the human race and join this super-species. I could do it simply by clasping her in my arms. What firm but responsive breasts!

"I'd like to see her a minute."

"Who are you? I am Mrs. Foulkes."

I still didn't understand this smashing bird was my aunt and said, "I'm her nephew, Mr. Foulkes's nephew, over for the war."

Her eyes showed a lot of white at that. The extra exposure was sensually provocative. Her teeth were trapped like little, clean, white blossoms under the parted lips. Between her eyebrows was a vertical line. I realised belatedly that she must have worn this expression of surprise and annoyance from the moment she clapped eyes on me. Quite evidently, she had been expecting somebody else.

"You're a liar!"

"Captain Foulkes is very ill." I spoke of him in this way because I still could not believe she was who she claimed to be. I imagined her passing on the information to the real Mrs. Foulkes.

"Clear off," she said, looking crosser than ever. She closed the door in my face and I could hear a chain rattling and a bolt being slid

Absurd as it may seem, my main thought was what a figure I must have cut in my army issue khaki shorts. These were the ones with flaps which could be unbuttoned and let down to be secured below the knees. The other chaps had either cut these flaps off or bought sporty-looking shorts, Big White Hunter style, that made them look like senile Boy Scouts. I alone had struck to my Shorts, Tropical, Fully-Flapped, Anti-Malarial, and they hung round my thighs like a quilted skirt. There are little tailors and laundries in the basement of every Cairo block. As soon as I had finished ringing the doorbell, hammering with my fist on the ironwork and shouting outside Aunt Nadia's flat – this lasted for some minutes – I went and found a tailor and offered him a pound if he would de-flap my shorts immediately. These are the very shorts I am wearing at this moment.

So far as the kit is concerned, the difference between what I wore then and what I wear now from time to time is the medal ribbons. We joked about gongs but these ribbons have proved unexpectedly important. I touch them. War Medal, red, white and blue; 1939–45 Star, red with dark blue and light blue stripe; France and Germany Star, blue, white and red stripe; most evocative of all, the unwatered ribbon of the Africa Star – predominantly pale buff, with a fine stripe of dark blue, a fine stripe of light blue; in the middle, a broad red stripe. But the predominant colour is officially pale buff, meant to be the colour of sand, no doubt, but gold in my vocabulary.

There was the day Uncle Raymond said he realised it was un-fashionable to admire a military adventurer like Alexander the Great. "But I've got to be honest. Anyway, he was a bit of a prig and that makes me warm to him too. Couldn't stand rape, for example. Cracked down on it. I could never actually see myself as an Alexander. One of his philosopher companions, perhaps, rebuking him for drinking too much. His friend Calanus, the naked Indian philosopher, must have done that. Calanus had himself sacrificed on a funeral pyre to the sound of trumpets and the trumpeting of elephants." Uncle Raymond looked serious, which meant that he grinned merrily. "In the right frame of mind I would be capable of such things, Tishy. Calanus said 'Bodies you can move about but souls you cannot compel.' Now, my soul cannot be compelled."

chapter 2

Cairo, before El Alamein, was bathed in innocence. That room in the Sharia Soleiman Pasha Y.M.C.A. faced east. As soon as the sun came up the minarets of the old city could be seen glittering in the morning light. Later the air would become dusty but before and soon after the sun sprang up behind those Mokattam heights it was empty, pure and cold. Night had washed it. The mosques were so clearly lit you had the illusion every grain in the stone they were built of could be identified. The sky was empty. It was so empty of cloud or fleck or flaw the sun seemed unsupported and precarious. All this clear brightness was intoxicating. If the appropriate piece of desert could be discovered, a man could walk naked into it, like Adam in the morning of the world. The innocence was entirely mine.

This was not something I knew at the time. It was spring, the almond trees in blossom in the streets, and the sun hot but not too hot. Cairo was a sanctuary. At night the lights blazed and the bombs did not come. Egypt itself was not at war. Cairo was neutral. The beggars, the shopkeepers, the *effendi*, the police in their tarbooshes, the droves of men in dark glasses playing trick-track in the vast cafés, the European-looking women in dress shops and Groppi's, the happy peasants on a flat-topped cart pulled by pewter donkeys, the veiled women in black who clapped hands rhythmically and laughed and screamed as they went by on one of the open trams, they were all neutral and safe, it seemed. They were not standing on any slippery slope.

I telephoned Nadia from the Y.M.C.A. Fearing she might hang

up on me once she realised who was calling I said I was Captain Brown of the Pay Corps; I just wanted to know if she was receiving the right pay and allowances and at the right frequency. I mean, what with her husband being in hospital –

"Who is that speaking?" she said after I had been talking about NAAFI shopping facilities and the possibility Captain Foulkes's stay in hospital might affect his entitlement to Field Allowance. I had meant to sound both very official and at the same time concerned on her behalf.

"Captain Brown."

"You're the soldier who was round here yesterday. Why do you humiliate me?"

"Me?"

"You lie to me. You try to deceive me. Do you think I'm a fool?"

"I just thought you wouldn't talk if you knew who I was."

"Why should I be afraid of you?" She was shouting so much her voice cracked. "Very well, you can come and see me. I shall show you whether I am afraid of you and your family."

It did not surprise me when, just about to press the doorbell of Flat 3, I was attacked. It was a gloomy building. There was no artificial lighting in the staircase well and I simply had not noticed this man standing in the shadow to the right of the door even though I was expecting trouble. I was apprehensive mainly because the behaviour of Uncle Raymond and his wife was so odd and I was uncertain what to do. I had no interest in Uncle Raymond's marital troubles as such. If Aunt Nadia had not been so unexpectedly young and fetching I would not have pretended to be Captain Brown of the Pay Corps. So, the truth as I saw it, was that I stood in front of Aunt Nadia's door not because she was Aunt Nadia but because she had disturbed me sexually and that was enough to make the sort of young man I was feel guilty. Not morbidly guilty, because I still was not sure this girl really was what she claimed to be. But guilty enough, and uncertain enough, and sufficiently impressed by her anger, to know that if someone beat me up it was no less than I deserved.

It was a clumsy attack by a man who moved stiffly and beat at me with his fists while he made whimpering, baby noises. He appeared to be suffering and very sorry for himself. He was hatless. He wore a grey European-style suit, a shirt but no collar or tie. His jacket was unbuttoned and as he lifted his arms amateurishly high to pound me it parted to reveal braces of such bright red they stood out even in that half light. I punched him in the mouth just as the door of the flat opened. By the grating under my knuckles I guessed I had smashed his dentures.

Nadia, who was standing there, did not say anything. I did not say anything. We both looked down on this man sitting on his haunches with his back up against the wall. He was holding his mouth and moaning; an elderly man, seen more clearly now in the daylight that streamed through the open door, his grey socks around his ankles, his head bent forward so that we could see a silvery scalp through the thin hair. He was whimpering in much the same way as when he first came at me. Quite a thin man. At a guess, he would not have weighed more than ten stone. But he had scared me. I did not know whether he had a knife. Now that I was no longer scared I despised him. Poor stupid old crow!

Nadia looked at me. She was wearing a long fawn dress with lace at the collar. I could not see her face very clearly because the light was coming from behind. But I knew she was looking at me and I knew, from her silence and the way she now gazed down at this old crow, not moving, that she despised him too. I guessed she had a contemptuous look on her face. Her silence and immobility were hostile and pitiless; as I was hostile and pitiless. We were both aware, God knows how! the other had precisely this contempt for the broken old chap – blood coming out of his mouth now – and first she laughed and then I laughed. She excited me because she was standing so close, laughing and smelling of something lemony but sweet. We were drawn together by our obvious lack of pity. Not cruelty. There was defiance in this pitiless way we were laughing; as much as to say, we'll be broken some day and all we'll expect in our turn will be pitiless laughter too. We don't want your love or understanding or mercy.

21

Once in the flat with the door closed I said, "He just went for me."

"He often does that," she said.

"You know him?"

"He's my father."

It was a reception room with a low marble-topped table in the middle, a settee and chairs covered in what looked like white cotton ranged round the walls, a large coloured photograph of King Farouk on one side of the room and another of the main administrative block of Reading University on the other.

She was mad as a ferret. That was why she ignored Uncle Raymond and hated her father. She looked nothing like a ferret. She had a rather round face with full lips, not much colour in her cheeks and a small nose, wide at the base. Her very dark hair hung in two loose but very stylish knots on either side of a lot of white throat. She looked more like the Sphinx. She had that chubby, cat-like look but she put me in mind of a ferret because I had seen one with blood on its mouth, fresh from a rabbit warren.

She noticed my knuckles were bleeding and sent me down to the bathroom to tidy up. Instead of entering the room where Nadia was waiting when I returned to the hall I opened the front door to look for the old man. There was no sign of him. I went down the two flights of stone steps to the main entrance from the street but there was nobody there either, only the porter in a filthy-looking gown sitting on a stool. When I returned to the flat Nadia was standing at the door. She wanted to know what I'd been up to.

"I was looking for that man. He wasn't really your father, was he?"

"Show me your army Pay Book so that I know who *you* really are." We went back into the reception room where a servant girl, just a child, in a long black cotton dress had delivered a tray bearing two coffee cups and a long handled brass pot with vapour rising from it. At Nadia's request I drew the shutters while she examined my Pay Book. The light reflected upwards from the Midan through the slats and everything in the room seemed to vibrate in a dusty white glow. Outside, the trams clanged by.

"It says here your name is Cozens, David Cozens."

"Uncle Raymond is my mother's brother. She was Miss Foulkes before she married. He's been very ill, your husband. If he is your husband. I mean, I expected someone a bit older."

"I was one of his students."

"He's very cut up." She did not seem to register anything about her husband's illness. "He was on the D.I. list," I said, "but he's O.K. now."

We drank coffee and she didn't say anything for some time after she handed the Pay Book back. She breathed rather noisily and quickly. It made her presence, in that peculiar light, so overpowering that I could not look at her though I was aware she was looking at me carefully.

"I'll be going back to the hospital. I'll be seeing Uncle Raymond so I'll say I've seen you and that you're all right, etcetera. Is there any message?"

"What sort of woman is his wife?"

"You said you were his wife."

"His wife in England."

"You mean Aunt Treasure," I said idiotically, forgetting the warnings Uncle Raymond had given me and indeed, forgetting whole chunks of the story about his first marriage. This was the effect of sitting close to Nadia in that shuttered room, listening to the coming and going of her breath, so close that I could have put out a hand and rested it on her right, uncovered knee. She wore smokey-coloured stockings and her knees appeared to be trembling. It was some optical trick induced by the weave of these stockings but it added to the general uncertainty.

"Is that a real name? Treasure?" Her face turned towards me but I couldn't look back.

"How did you know about her?"

"You think I went prying and searching. Why not? My family warned me. My friends warned me. I took no notice because I was stupid. They said Englishmen who could not go home to England for a long time often married foreign women, even though they had wives at home. Soldiers do it mostly. I didn't think university professors would."

She was Uncle Raymond's legal wife all right and my legal aunt too. I was belatedly remembering the Post Office engineer and the divorce. I ought to have said something about this but the information just stuck in my throat.

"Where were you married?"

"At the British Consulate."

"Didn't he have to produce a document or something?"

"The chaplain said Raymond Reginald Foulkes, bachelor, and he didn't say anything against that. I'd been waiting for him to say something because my friends said a man that age must have been married before."

Her English was very good, a better accent than mine if the truth were told. When she said a word like "before" with a round syllable in it her mouth became very round too. Ps and Bs were pronounced with a curious popping sound. She had been educated, I learned later, at the English Girls' School in Heliopolis and taught by women from Cheltenham Ladies' College and Girton.

Deeply treacherous, I now asked, "Why did you marry a man as old as that?"

What would Granny Foulkes have thought of her, sitting up at her cash desk in the greengrocer's shop, with her big jaw, her red hands (she wore woollen mittens in the winter; the fingers and thumbs stuck out of them like turkey talons) and her flat Midlands accent; what would she have thought of an Egyptian daughter-in-law, especially one like Nadia? It was like having a bird of paradise in the family.

"An arrangement was being made," Nadia said at last, "to marry me to a member of the Ethiopian royal family. They are all savages in that country. A girl is not safe from dangers like that until she is married."

"You'd have been royal yourself, then, so to speak?"

"They are Christians in Ethiopia but they are savages. I should have been a princess." She said this in a very prim, superior sort of way. To be a princess was something, no doubt, but she was Nadia, and that was better.

I believed all this. "You married Uncle Raymond so as not to marry this prince?"

"You don't understand. You think Mr. Foulkes a funny old man. I loved him."

This made me jealous. I said, "You couldn't possibly."

"Of course, I knew all the time he was despicable and a liar."

"How old are you?"

"Age doesn't matter."

"How old are you?"

"Older than you. You remind me of Mr. Foulkes. I expect you've been lying to me too. If I'd really been married to Mr. Foulkes that would make you my nephew, wouldn't it? But you are not. I don't even believe you are Mr. Foulkes's nephew."

"You said that man out there was your father."

"Yes."

"He often did that, attack people?"

"Yes."

"Why?"

She shrugged. "He waits for them and attacks them sometimes. What business is it of yours? I think you should go now."

I let myself out and left without saying goodbye, pretty angry. First of all she had involved me in a conspiracy at her father's expense (if he was her father) so that I felt confident of a close and even intimate relationship; then I had been rejected. But you could not have a relationship with somebody as crazy as Nadia.

I became damn sure that man was not her father. It would be quite incredible for a father to wait outside his daughter's flat and attack people who came to see her. I'd heard everybody in Egypt took hashish. He was just doped to the eyes. What kind of sickness caused her to claim him as a father? She just *wanted* a father. That was why she married Uncle Raymond. She wanted him as a father too. You could not be angry with a woman as sick as that. She had really cut me, castrated me if you like. She was an old man's girl. I saw myself as a castrated and adolescent non-combatant in a world that was all set to do me down. With an aunt like that who needed a psychiatrist?

That evening I went drinking with Q.M.S. Razier. We were in touch because I had phoned to ask him whether he could use his influence and winkle me out of the Medical Corps. Our talk ended with Razier calling for a taxi and taking me off to the red light district near the railway station. It was Out of Bounds, he said, and you had to keep a look out for Military Police who had a habit of patrolling the area from time to time. Razier said he had a duty to a young soldier. He was married himself and utterly faithful to his wife. From time to time, though, he went to a sex show in a brothel to be reminded what a nauseating, disgusting business sex was and how right he was to be utterly faithful to his wife. He wanted me to share his disgust so that in the months, and possibly years, I would spend in the armoured car unit to which he had promised to get me transferred, I would think of sex with the kind of loathing that would keep me as pure as he was. The technique, he explained, was one adopted by the Roman Church in the training of priests.

There was no show I can remember. We went up a wooden staircase that groaned with our weight and entered a badly lit room stinking of old tobacco smoke and sweet scent. Girls in belly-dancing kit were sitting about on low divans. There were two other soldiers there. They were drinking beer and talking quietly to girls who were lying back in very relaxed postures on cushions. It was a bit like hospital visiting. But where were the little presents and the bunches of grapes on the bedside table? The ward orderly would be coming in with the tea trolley. The subdued conversation and the general air of enforced politeness or calm in the face of something more violent unobtrusively going on elsewhere, made me feel this was a hospital all right. But Razier plainly did not see it that way. He was laughing and offering nips of scotch to the girls from a flask he had surprisingly produced. Perhaps he had been carrying it all the time and I had not noticed. I had a nip too.

One of the girls reminded me, a bit, of Nadia. She had the

26

same broad cheeks and full lips. She noticed I had observed her. After a while she took me by the hand and led me along a passage to a room so small there was space only for the divan and a three-legged iron table on which burned an old-fashioned oil lamp, with a flowered bowl, a funnel and a globe like the full moon. I remember the smell of this lamp and her sweat. First she removed her brassière and trousers. She helped me to undress. Naked we stood and looked at each other, smiling. I had never seen a girl naked before and was put off by the discoloured nipples like watching eyes on her small, hanging breasts. I had never made love to a girl. Unexpectedly, she kissed me lightly on the right shoulder, then my left, caressing me gently and lovingly with her lips. She suddenly dropped to her knees and lifting my stiffening penis with the index finger of her right hand she kissed that too. The pity, the love, the gentleness, the reassurance of the gesture turned the day inside out. You will never be despised or sneered at here, she seemed to be saying. You are what you are! You are young and strong. Rejoice in your youth and manliness.

"Fife buns!" Her English was almost non-existent. She held up her right hand and crooked her fingers and thumb in sequence.

I fished my wallet out of the back pocket of my trousers but I had lodged Uncle Raymond's money in the Y.M.C.A. safe, all except three pounds and after the night out with Q.M.S. Razier there were only two of these left. I offered them. She took the wallet as well and examined it, monkey-like, to make sure I was not cheating. When she knew I was not she returned the wallet and just one of the notes. The other she held between her teeth while she put her pants on again.

"Fife buns. Only for fife buns." She said this kindly and, I fancied, with regret. She shrugged her bony shoulders and, naked as I was, I actually helped her to do up her brassière at the back. I understood perfectly. The rules of the house could not be broken and she had taken one pound as a sort of fine, for the trouble I had caused. Even this was managed without the kind of resentment that might have sapped the self-confidence she had given me. She liked me! She was very sorry! That's all.

She was nowhere in sight by the time I dressed and clumped back to the main salon. Razier was not to be seen either so I guessed he was undergoing the aversion therapy he had told me about. No need, as I saw it, to handicap myself like that. The whore had made me bigger, tougher and a lot kinder than came naturally. By kissing my prick she took away shame from it. The encounter with Nadia put me down, diminished, emasculated me. Now I was virile again, poor bastard!

Strangely enough, the smell of this tropical kit after it has been laundered (I sit here unshaven but the uniform is clean) prompts the almost-forgotten stirring in the loins. The smell is biscuity, because the kit is lightly starched before the hot iron is passed over it, something the modern laundry would never dream of doing. So I do it myself. My *madeleine!* After twenty-five years the shirt and shorts are the same, which only goes to show how exercise can keep the weight down. Scorched starch in the nostrils and the ineffectual lickerish promptings come again.

In bed with Nadia I heard her say – well, what? God! the rubbish that woman talked when all that mattered was the flesh! The great crime so far as she was concerned, was illusion and self-deception. She said, "There is a Marxist explanation. It would go as follows. I am angry with Professor Foulkes because I am an exploited colonial and he is the imperialist aggressor. No Copt would believe that. We are too much weighed upon by the Moslems to believe that. I'm just angry with Professor Foulkes because he is a liar. He's destroyed my sexual self-respect. What next? Being in bed with you. Or anyone. If he had said, 'Be my mistress,' that is something I could have considered. It makes sense and I am sensible. But he didn't even have the respect for me that would enable him to put a realistic question. He just took it for granted he could deceive me. An Egyptian in England could do the same to an Englishwoman. It's nothing to do with imperialism. We are just life's prey when we talk like that. Raymond is very interested in Alexander the Great. He is writing a monograph. He told me Alexander thought he was a hero in a poem. But I look at things as they are."

"With anyone?" Surely, in an outraged tone, I must have said that.

"Anyone," she said. "You can't totally strip a woman of her self-respect."

I went into Uncle Raymond's cubicle to report. He was not in his bed, though it looked as though he might well have just got out of it. But he was not to be seen. He was still so weak he ought to be using a bed pan; there was no question of his going out to the latrines. He wasn't in the ward. I went out by the west entrance and saw a figure in blue hospital pyjamas moving away through the sun dazzle, dragging a hard shadow. He turned, saw me, waved and went on again, up the slope, as much to say, "Don't tell me! I can't bear to know."

"You shouldn't be out here," I said when I caught up with him. "You'll get the orderly shoved on a charge."

"I'm all right, Tishy. Look!" He sat on a packing case and waved a hand westward like the old sailor in the *Boyhood of Raleigh*. "See that wall and the trees?"

He was not bare-footed, as I had supposed. He wore a pair of the local sandals, just toe-cap and sole. The fact that the blue pyjamas and the yellow sandals were all that stood between him and total nakedness did not matter because it was hot. We had to screw up our eyes in the brilliance. It came up at us from the sand. He still had not shaved. In that glare the only positive colour was provided by his blue pyjamas and his sandals; his thin, tapering beard, his face, lined and mask-like after his illness, and the fuzz of bright hair over the big head – all these were colourless to the point of transparency. I guessed he had heard me come into the ward, recognised my voice when I spoke to the orderly, and immediately beat it out into the desert because he funked hearing what I thought of Aunt Nadia and what she was up to.

"She's O.K.," I said, to put him out of his misery. "I saw her. She's fine."

"That wall and those trees," he said, after a short pause, his voice trembling. "You see them? That's the Military Cemetery of Tel el-Kebir. The battle of 1881. British lads there in foreign earth. When I am stronger you and I will walk over there and pay our tribute."

"You might have told me she was just a girl."

"And down there," he went on, "where you see all that green and the palm trees, is the course of the Sweetwater Canal. It was built to convey drinking water from the Nile when the Suez Canal was built. This is the Land of Goshen, where the Israelites lived."

"She looked fine to me. You didn't say she was young."

He sobbed. At least, I took that strangled grunt to be a sob. He waved his right arm again. We were on what passed for an eminence in that flat desert. We would see down to the culti- vated green along the Sweetwater Canal. To the north, too, quivering in the heat and apparently half way up the sky was a little white cupola and a line of palms. South, were toy moun- tains made of crinkled cardboard. "Tishy, if you looked at all this very closely you'd see evidence for a major part of the his- tory of the human race. There are only two choices. Everybody who's walked these parts knew that. Either you take the initia- tive or you go to ground. Like a badger."

"If you're seen out here there'll be trouble."

"That's all right, Tishy. They wouldn't be hard on a convales- cent officer."

"Put your arm round my neck."

In that dry heat you did not sweat much but he had me sweating before we had covered half the distance back to the ward. He was so weak he just had to lean on me and in spite of the way his illness had emaciated him he was still a big and heavy man. A Q.A. came out of the marquee and saw us. She was a claret-faced Irishwoman who immediately began roaring. "Private Cozens, what do you think you're doing with that officer?"

We got him back to bed and the orderly was told to give him a blanket bath. Quite what Uncle Raymond had in mind when he talked of the alternative choices, either taking the initiative or going to ground, I had no idea – subsequently he was to explain it by saying his great heroes were Alexander the Great and St.

30

Antony the well-known recluse – but I supposed it had something to do with Aunt Nadia. If I never mentioned her name again I suspected he wouldn't bring the subject up. The information he wanted about her was deliberately limited. I had communicated everything he wanted to know. She was alive and well. He didn't want to hear any more. He was too scared. The truth was he knew as well as I did that she was crazy. He didn't want it spelled out. The effect was to make me wonder whether the family was right about book learning, more particularly the view that if you were not brought up to it and it was not your right, so to speak, by virtue of the class you belonged to, then all that reading might come between you and reality.

Nadia's letter arrived soon after and this raises an important question of procedure. The letter no longer exists. Certainly, I've no copy of it. Vivid though the impression was it made on me there can be no guarantee, when I try to reproduce it, I've got more than its general line and tone right. The guts of the thing is true. The guts of this whole thing is true. Sweating and straining to dredge back as much of the Nadia affair as possible I find it all comes up smelling of truth. If it didn't the whole point of the exercise would be lost, which is to prove things happened in the way I say they did. All right, you sharpen up the detail and even invent when you don't remember precisely what was said, or how it happened, or where. No therapist disciplines me. Words discipline me. The need to present everything in proper order disciplines me. What I leave out disciplines me. Out of the disciplines comes the assurance the past existed, that there is colour where if you believe some people was an unrefracting void, that a lie wouldn't be so consistent, and that I have set beating an old heart.

The letter to Uncle Raymond must have gone something like this:

"The young soldier who came said you were better and I was glad to hear it because you know how much I hate disease and hospitals and death. You deserve death but though I would say that to your face I would not put it into writing. It is impossible for me to visit you, so cease troubling me on that score. I do not like hospitals and I do not like to make enquiries about people who are ill in case the news is bad. The smell of hospitals is upsetting. I cannot set foot in one. In spite of everything I am glad you make a recovery so well, because you are after all a human being and I should be glad to have more news of you. Your own presence would upset me but if the young soldier called in person I should be interested to know how you are progressing.

"The Company is writing to you about the rent. I do not understand matters like that, nor do I wish to. The young soldier must telephone before calling, otherwise I might be out."

There was a lot about practical matters – repairs to the balcony, electricity and phone bills, and the like. But this is pretty well how the letter would have been. Setting it down is to hear again the way she talked, as though her nose were a bit stuffed up, with popping Ps and Bs. She appeared sarcastic or ironical when in fact nothing of the sort was intended. She claimed always to say what was in her mind, meaning she didn't adapt her remarks to the company. But I also took it to mean she was committed to all the views she expressed and that surely must have been a pose. Nobody could be that outrageous, but it later turned out that she at any rate could be; and when she was apparently ribbing Uncle Raymond in this letter by implying her dislike of hospitals was more important than any concern for him, this was not a ribbing at all. She really was upset by hospitals. It really did rule out a visit. That, and other things, ruled it out too; and even the other things she hadn't burked.

After his relapse Uncle Raymond had been so ill he had been transferred to the Military Hospital in Ismailia which was brick-built and had doors. It was when I called on him there that he showed me this letter from Nadia, absolutely delighted because it was the first word he had received from her since falling ill and he gave me all the credit. I was bowled over because I could see it was a straight invitation to call again. Not knowing my address Nadia had written to Uncle Raymond on the assumption he would show it to me. My own news for Uncle Raymond was that Q.M.S. Razier had done what he could and that was not much. Instead of a posting to the Infantry Training Base at Abbassia – which would have needed authorisation by the Director of Medical Services back in England – I was transferred to H.Q., British Troops in Egypt to train as a clerk, which was the last thing I wanted.

"Wonderful!" said Uncle Raymond. His drawn face actually took on a little colour. He grasped my hand. "Ah – ah – ah!" He gasped and wheezed. "You'll be in Cairo. You'll see Nadia. You'll keep in touch. You'll let me know how she is."

H.Q. office troops slept in huts set up in a garden not five minutes' walk from the Midan Ismailia and no sooner had I dumped my kit than I wandered off in that direction. It was night. Everything in sight seemed edible. Lights were butter or honey, a mosque was white cheese and the rough trunks of palm trees crusty like well-baked bread.

In the flat such a party was going on the music and laughing could be heard on the pavement below, audible through the traffic noises and drowned only by a tram as it shuddered and clanked past. The windows were open, lights blazed out and people were standing on the two balconies.

It was Nadia's flat all right because when I climbed the stairs and rang the bell the noise was coming from the other side of that familiar glass-fronted door. A gramophone or radio was playing "South of the Border", people were joining in the chorus, and a girl was laughing. The door opened and there stood an R.A.F. officer with little bands of blue in the epaulettes of his khaki shirt and a single wing so I knew he was a navigator or a bomb aimer, or something short of being a pilot. I was vague about the R.A.F. because we all thought they had let us down at Calais.

"Come in, friend." He was so drunk he would have fallen down if he hadn't leaned on the door.

"Bugger off, son!" said a harassed-looking major who appeared behind him and tried to shut the door. The noise was pretty deafening and he had to shout to make himself heard.

"Is Mrs. Foulkes in?" was all I could think to say.

33

"What's that?" He pushed past the R.A.F. chap and I could see he was itching to get his fingers on me. "This is Officers Only in here."

Nadia appeared, quite stunning in a long white dress and her hair done up on top of her head with little white flowers, jasmine I think. She had a glass in her hand.

"It's you, is it?" she said in a tight, hard little voice and I could see she was angry too. That made two of them, the major and Nadia, standing there side by side and just wanting me off the premises. "You were told to telephone first."

"Aren't you going to invite me in, Auntie?" I said.

"Bloody cheek, eh? Beat it, son. Or I'll be wanting your unit, name and number." The major sweated with rage. "How many times have you got to be told?"

"Who are these people, Aunt Nadia?"

Uncle Raymond would have wanted me to be firm. "Go right in, Tishy," I could imagine him saying. "Order them out."

Everybody thought in military terms in those days. The flat was occupied territory. In the name of Uncle Raymond, I had to establish myself there and get these men out. Nothing so intimately challenging had happened to me before. I wasn't forgetting Calais but at Calais nobody laughed at me. Here every remark it occurred to me to make sounded risible.

The major and the drunken navigator and Nadia and an amazed Berber who appeared in a brilliant white turban carrying a tray of coffee, all these, and myself, and the smell of cooking fat and the clank and splutter of trams (their wheels screamed in the rails as they came round the sharp turn from Bab el Louk), all these can be reassembled. But it is just a false stage effect unless you remember the future is what the past has not got when you recreate it. I thought I was *en route* for some state where all would be justified and the meaning made clear. There is no such journey. The mêlée of Midan Ismailia was an end in itself. I might have said, Enjoy this for what it is. The point of being alive is not your death bed. I must have been readier to run away than I'd supposed at the time.

"What's he call you auntie for?" The flight lieutenant put an arm round my neck. "He's a decent good-looking boy, if you ask me, and there must be some reason, I find him quite charming. Come and have a drink." He was a real Irish pansy.

I was inside the flat drinking sour white wine under the photograph of Reading University. The major had temporarily lost interest in me and was dancing with a dark-skinned fattish woman I hadn't seen before. After a while Nadia came over and said, "You looked terrified."

"Uncle Raymond's ill and I don't know what he'd think of all this."

"Why don't you ask me to dance?"

"Send all these people away."

"What!" I had remained seated. I was damned if I was going to stand up for her. She stood there, looking down at me, annoyed and superior so I reached up, caught her by the wrists and dragged her down until she was sitting on my knees.

"Uncle Raymond's a good man. He's a saint." (I was so sexually excited I was talking wildly. Every slight movement as our bodies adjusted to each other was erotic. She had me slavering.) "I know he divorced Aunt Treasure. He is your legal husband. I've got to speak up for him."

"And put your hand up my dress?"

I withdrew it. "Well, I'm fond of him," I said, as though this was an explanation for the way I had, as in a trance, been exploring, right up to the tightly fitting knickers.

"In this country," she said, "women observe a strict code of morals. If they break the code their brothers kill them. All the sin is on the woman, not the man. I will carry no man's sin for him. You understand?"

She jumped to her feet and pushed back the major who had noticed her situation and broken off his dancing to come and rescue her. The flight lieutenant was winding up the gramophone which had been slowly running down. He was repeating to himself, in some surprise, "He called her auntie, just now."

"It's all right," she said to the major. "The party must finish or there'll be complaints from the neighbours. This is a quiet building. You must all go."

"Not without that shit." The major pointed at me. "There's something funny going on."

"I'll tell you what it is." She was in a temper again. Her eyes widened and actually seemed to glitter. She raised her right arm and, like a bad actress, pointed a drooping finger at me with a scarlet nail at the end of it. "I am that boy's uncle's whore."

There was a certain amount of laughter at this and people gathered round to see what was going on. The R.A.F. pansy clapped in an uncomprehending way and Nadia turned on him.

"You think it comes easily for me to say such a disgraceful thing."

He was confused. "I was just registering appreciation of that chap's face." He was looking at me. "He looked marvellous in a tortured sort of way."

Before I could shut Nadia up she had plunged into an account of her marriage and how she had discovered Uncle Raymond's deception. She had been the best student in her year and if it had not been for the war could have expected to go to England to take a higher degree. Marrying Professor Foulkes was the next best thing. At least she got away from her family.

"No, that is not true," she cried out, as though someone had contradicted her; whereas everyone was quiet. I was outraged. Family confidences should not be brought into the open like this. She made drama out of her marriage and performed it in public. If Nadia had been in Aunt Treasure's position she would have set up a booth in the High Street and told everybody about this marvellous Post Office engineer from the West Midlands. I saw England as a private sort of country with lots of mysteries. In Egypt there were none.

Nadia had this aristocratic way of bringing everything into view. If she had an ache in her fanny she'd have wanted to show you the place. I had a picture of her standing like a conjurer pulling endless coloured streamers out of her mouth, streamers

36

of intimate truth, coloured confessional streamers of money talk, sex talk, talk without shame or reticence, because she assumed that everybody else was much the same as she was and she saw no reason to keep her trap shut about the human condition.

She stood and harangued us. She waved away objections with her right hand. She stabbed the air. She brought her right fist down into the palm of her left hand and declaimed literary English. "I always had my suspicions. I had my suspicions before the so-called ceremony. I overcame them. I was stupid. I was intent on getting away from my family. They are so suffocating. Raymond is a fascinating man and clever and strong and paternal. But he is a liar and he has disgraced me because he is such a good man and a strong lover. He brought me shame and humiliation. I no longer respect myself. He has destroyed me."

She looked round at the major, the Irish flight lieutenant, the podgy dark-skinned woman, and the rest, daring them to contradict her.

I said to the major in a low voice, "You can see she is not well. Actually, she is my aunt by marriage. Her husband, my uncle, is an officer in the Canal Defence Corps."

"I will tell you all," said Nadia, very loud, "how I discovered my shame." Now that she had cottoned on to it she enjoyed my embarrassment. "I found an old postal package in a box – stamped, unopened and addressed to Mrs. Raymond Foulkes from England. The stamps bore the head of King George the Fifth who died when I was sixteen years old. It was not possible!"

"What was in the package?" The major was interested all of a sudden.

"A pair of razor blades. Old-fashioned open razors, I mean."

"What would a woman want with razors?"

"Some women have to shave," said the plump woman without taking the cigarette out of her mouth.

"These razors," said Nadia, "were in a presentation box and it was clear from the letter accompanying them they were intended as a surprise birthday present – from the recipient, who was a Mrs. Foulkes!"

"I meant to say, that's the thought that was going through my head, you know," said the major. "You couldn't be sure it was Mrs. and not Mr. on the label of that package. It might have been a smudge. It could have been a typing error."

"Inside the presentation box was a letter beginning 'Dear Madam'. She had ordered the razors and was going to give them to Raymond as a present. That was how I knew Raymond had been married before and that his wife is in England at this minute. I tried to cut my throat and slash my wrists." She extended her left wrist and we saw a silver scar about two inches long.

"When?"

"Three months ago."

"It doesn't make sense to me," I said, "an unopened postal package hanging about all these years. Anyway, nobody uses an open razor these days."

"If you say he divorced this first wife why did he not tell me instead of pretending he was a bachelor?"

"He could not bear you to know. It would make him lose face."

"You're a bigger fool than you look," said Nadia.

This was before I bought myself a pair of decent low shoes. I wore the heavy army issue boots and short puttees so I was able to stamp my way out of the flat with some effect. Nadia, though, caught me up on the stairs and slipped her arm into mine, so naturally and easily I picked up her hand in mine and found it cool, small and delicate.

"I told you to telephone before coming. Believe me," she said intimately and trustingly, with her head close to mine, "the marriage is not valid." In contrast with her oratorical manner back in the flat her voice was low; I could smell the jasmine and feel her shape pressing against my side. She was just three inches shorter than me, and I knew she just wanted to touch me and I wanted to touch her; so our hips touched and our shoulders touched but because she was just that much shorter than I was we seemed to fit that much better. I could slip an arm round her waist and lift her up slightly.

"Perhaps the war will never end. I shall kill myself if it goes on too long. I can't live without self-respect."

"What do you need for that?"

"A real, legal husband." She might have been proposing to me there and then. If Uncle Raymond, as a member of a certain English family, had destroyed her self-respect, then another member of that family could restore it. I stood there with my right hand actually caressing her right breast, fuddled by her sexuality.

"It is terrible to be young and have a man throw you away like a sucked orange." This was of a piece with the come-hither letter. "But I'm exacting retribution," she called down to me quaintly, tossing her head and looking hard-done by, as she went back up the stairs to the open door of the flat where, judging by the row, the party had started again.

Not being invented, this account is nevertheless coloured by professional fiction and that is to be resented. The writers have let us down. Nobody can live up to the vitality of fiction. It leaves us feeling inadequate. The novelists have affected the norm. Life, as they show it, is nymphomaniac. We can't go on being raped by the literary imagination – poor, frustrating, deliberately compensatory as it is for the emasculated loneliness of the writer. But it is the only available technique for remembering. Uncle Raymond turned my attention to the Desert Fathers. For the first time in history, he said, behaviour nowadays is dictated not by the preachers nor the educationists nor by hard circumstance, but by the literary entertainers. In the absence of any real equivalent to modern novels and drama what possibly could have driven those good men out into the desert?

Curious that Nadia and St. Antony were racially linked. He could be a remote uncle.

chapter 3

Colonel Patch was the Assistant Director of Medical Services, British Troops in Egypt, and when the news came through that Hitler had invaded Russia he said that any stick – meaning the Soviet Union – was good enough to beat a dog with – meaning Hitler. The Germans had come into Egypt through Halfaya Pass two months before. We were out of Crete by this time. It seemed a good moment to say something like, "I'm in the Medical Corps by mistake and I'd like to apply for transfer to a combatant unit."

He had an office in the Semiramis Hotel overlooking the Nile which was so wide at the southern end of Gezireh that it looked like a lake. The sun shone, the river was a brown luxury in the midsummer heat and I thought of the scene on Calais pier when the rumour broke that Jerry had invaded Russia. The sun was shining then, too, and I lay on the bleached boards too exhausted to wipe another man's blood from my face.

"Cozens," said Colonel Patch, "don't push your luck." But some time later I was sent for and told I was going on a course with the Camel Corps.

It turned out to be not the Camel Corps but a unit of the Long Range Desert Group in the dunes on the other side of the Pyramids. Ten miles or so west of Gizeh there was a real feeling of being out in the blue. This unit was made up of spares from the 10th Hussars and the Armoured Corps who fancied themselves as Mark II Lawrences of Arabia striking terror behind the German lines; but for the most part training seemed to consist of driving jeeps into soft sand and digging them out again.

We had netting and painted canvas for camouflage, we lived on biscuit, bully and a couple of pints of slightly salt water a day. My job was medical orderly. The Medical Officer and I had a covered jeep indistinguishable from the others, no Red Cross, and we got to know each other well.

Men in the L.R.D.G. were allowed to grow beards. Major Mc-Kellar soon looked every bit the hairy clansman. He was a territorial. As a very young man he had served in the ranks of the Black Watch in the First War, then qualified in medicine and played rugger for Scotland. When I knew him he was mainly interested in hammer throwing. He had won prizes at the Highland Games and wanted to win more when the war was over, in spite of being well up in his forties. He improvised a hammer by wiring together a couple of house bricks he had picked up in Cairo, securing them to a four-foot length of steel cable and making a grip for his hands by wrapping yards of surgical plaster round this steel cable.

His throwing was erratic. There were complaints from the rest of the unit when these house bricks and steel cable came whistling among them, sometimes separately, because the hammer had a way of disintegrating in mid air. He therefore felt obliged to go some way off into the desert and as he had a terror of getting lost he used to post me on top of a dune from where I could see both him and the encampment. He explained that after whirling round and round to throw the hammer he had absolutely no sense of direction.

"You're just a young laddie," he said to me after one of these late afternoon bouts of hammer throwing, "much as I was a young laddie in the other war. And d'you know what I think about life? Somehow I've missed all the fun. And when I say fun I mean sin. There it is. It's too late now. Sulphanilamides and contraception have taken all the sin out of fornication."

After a week or so of digging jeeps out of soft sand Major McKellar said he had run out of essential medical supplies and took me off to dinner one Friday evening in Mena House Hotel. He lent me one of his old shirts with three captain's pips on the shoulders because the place was Officers Only. He said he didn't want me embarrassed. An acquaintance of his, a spindly, boss-eyed colonel on the General Staff bought us some beer and said I looked young to be medically qualified. Having been introduced as Captain Cozens of No. 3 Field Ambulance I had to lie about my age. The place was full of top brass. There were quite a few women in uniform and a scattering of civilian women. "Jewesses and Greeks by the look of them," said McKellar knowingly.

When the Colonel had gone I said, "Would you mind if we split up? There's a girl coming out from Cairo and I didn't tell her I wasn't alone."

McKellar was delighted. "I'll see you at the jeep about one." (It was then ten o'clock.) "I don't want to be later than that."

He did not ask about the girl, or how I had managed to make contact with her at such short notice, but went off to the bar still laughing, and exuding approval. That's the way to live, my boy! False pips, a bit of skirt and a booze-up. It's 1917 again. Gather ye rosebuds. Give me pranks to regret and tendernesses to remember! Stretch me, God, on the delicious rack of the world! Test me! Expose me! Even now it is not too late. He staggered slightly because the colonel had presented him with a bottle of scotch before leaving, and we had been drinking it; he walked uncertainly, eyeing the A.T.S. girls and the Greek and Jewish women with a guarded wantonness. Later, he would want me to tell him all about my adventures with this girl from Cairo. But not now. His imagination was caught by the possibility of adventure and he did not want to be brought to earth by anything that underlined the fact that the adventure was not his, that it was not 1917, that he was no longer young, and that until his time came which, as it turned out, was to be not long, at El Alamein, eyeing the girls lewdly would be as far as he'd get.

If youth knew; if age could. What that leaves out is that age can forget. The experience of youth becomes remote and implausible, and that's why the young and randy are sometimes shocked by the way the elderly make light of sex, using words like "boring" about porn. There comes a stage – McKellar didn't live long enough to know this – when sex becomes implausible to the point of absurdity. There must have been anchorites at the end of long lives who were uneasy about the mortifications of the flesh they had practised when young. Had it all really been necessary? Uncle Raymond would probably have surmised that St. Antony's last torment was forgetting the strength of his many temptations and wondering whether his resistance had been on the extravagant side. In St. Antony's book that would be the sin of pride. It is easy to imagine Uncle Raymond speculating along these lines because I do it myself now that, unlike McKellar's recollections of 1917, I remember the youth I was with almost as much incredulity as if he'd been a cannibal. Did I ever eat human flesh? Or make love? Or was loved?

Well, yes. There must be some explanation for the feeling something is missing. This unflourishing dryness must have a case history. The knowledge it's dry and unflourishing here-abouts must indicate there was once a time of plenty; and that when the girl said "Fife buns" she really did give me a bit of my body, and that from Nadia I received a quite uncovenanted flowering of the flesh.

When her taxi arrived I was waiting on the steps. She would not let me help her. I opened the door of the taxi but she waved me aside when I tried to take her arm. She was wearing a long, shining, white dress that looked blue in the moonlight.

"I know the management. I've booked a room. It's too far to go back to Cairo tonight. Why couldn't you ring at a more civilised time? You expect me to come out at your beck and call." This angry excitement – and it was misplaced anger, be-cause I had phoned at about eight, which was a reasonable enough time for anyone, and I'd certainly made no suggestion she might come out to Gizeh – made me angry too. And the effect of this anger was sexually stimulating but cruel as well, as though we had known each other a long time, and were involved in a bloody conspiracy.

"So you're a captain now, dear Cozens." She never called me anything but Cozens. It was voluptuous and hostile at the same time. No woman had ever called me Cozens before except a schoolmistress who used to hit me with a ruler; Nadia called me

43

Cozens in bed, and that really used to bring out whatever brutality I was capable of. This may have been her intention. I don't know whether she knew the difference to a man, particularly an Englishman, between being called by his Christian and surname. Maybe she did. She was clever.

"Promoted on the field of battle," I explained. "I was given the choice – a commission or a crate of beer."

We drank a bottle of harsh Cyprus wine sitting in wicker chairs on the terrace looking east to the lights of the city under a mad-making full moon. She told me that Uncle Raymond had been home. He sent his love. He was now in Suez, attached to the Embarkation Officer. This was the sort of cushy job they would give to an officer who had just recovered from a serious illness. I said I was glad to hear about it but Nadia was noncommittal.

"How is he looking?" I asked.

"Awful. I only saw him for your sake."

"What do you mean?"

"Oh, you know. He's done this bad thing to me but he loves you and I thought if I could do a bad thing to you –" she was giggling; this was all a joke, but I didn't giggle – "I'd be getting my revenge. Why does he call you Tishy? You're attractive, Cozens. Did you know that? Have you a girl? No? You know nothing of girls?" She pouted and lifted her chin, just to show she was merely striking an attitude. Or maybe she wasn't. "You don't know what women are made of? So it would be a public service to show you, wouldn't it? Don't say I haven't warned. Come."

"That would be incest or something, wouldn't it? I mean, you're my aunt."

"I am not a woman," she said. "I am the real Sphinx. Look!" Sitting in her wickerwork chair she leaned forward into the moonlight and lifted her face where the wan evening of moths and flower scents seemed to hold it like a mask. She had the full lips and cheeks of the Sphinx. The real stone one was about half a mile away to the right of where we were sitting. "All around is the sacred dust of my ancestors. I am a Coptic Egyptian. We Copts are children of the dynasties. Have you seen the Sphinx? It was hewn by a silly artisan. He was trying to represent an idea in stone. He was not very clear-headed or experienced so the idea was badly carried out. He gave the Sphinx the face of a man. When the Greeks came to make Sphinxes they knew the real, old wisdom, older than the Gizeh Sphinx, and gave them the head and face of a woman. I know all this. I am that woman, Cozens. I am older than Sphinxes."

Calais taught the lesson, don't be a victim too long or the mind turns to mush. It is easier now to make the connection between war and love than it was in the Egyptian moonlight; but even if I'd understood at the time Nadia would still have over-run the defences. She had exotic force. It was irresistible. An Atlantic islander was sitting with excitement in his belly, certainly not thinking of history but reminded a bit out of his folk memory how little wine or lore or teaching he had of his own and that it had come from the sun and the east, from over the hills and far away. Nadia didn't know this. She didn't know her strength. She just thought she was rousing me – which she was, too.

"The real Sphinx does not ask riddles. It answers them. Like this." She lifted my hand and kissed it.

When she learned that Major McKellar would be waiting for me at the jeep at 1 a.m. and I'd have to be away by that time, she said I did not know who I was, I didn't know I existed. In my cold little mind, she went on, I had no apprehension of the scale against which the human condition had to be judged. Or something of that sort. This went on all the way to the bedroom where she rapidly divested herself of her clothes, instructed me to do the same, and then began touching me with the cold tips of her fingers, saying, "This is your nose. This is your left ear. This is your left shoulder bone. Under here are your ribs. Your heart is under this cage of bone. Your pelvic girdle encompasses your entrails, these the testicles that play a part in the creation of life and this absurdly dangling pipe is the channel of lust. At the very root of life is lust and pleasure. Do you understand that, Cozens? Be aware of yourself! Love me."

45

I stood to attention as if on parade. She was naming parts like a rifle instructor. Young soldier that I was, I thought the ultimate revelation was that God worked through a military manual and the riddle the Sphinx would now answer was to do with making love by numbers. What hardens in heat and softens in frost? Her tits stood out like not totally inflated sausage balloons with big nipples.

I woke up to find it was getting light and excited chattering coming from somewhere outside. Nadia was not in bed. I went and had a cold shower, feeling so relaxed and at the same time vigorous I could have worked miracles. That was the feeling. I could have up-ended Cheops' Pyramid. How strange! Incomprehensible! I returned to the bedroom towelling myself, expecting Nadia to have reappeared from somewhere; but not only did this not happen but I now saw her clothes had gone too. The bedroom faced east. I pulled back the gauzy curtains and saw the empty clarity of sky where the sun was coming up. I was still floating. My body glowed. I wanted to pat and stroke it. Why wasn't Nadia there to kiss it again? McKellar would have gone long ago. I dressed, putting on my shirt with the captain's pips.

Downstairs, when I got there, was more activity than you would expect at sun-up. The hall porter was telephoning. Two Egyptian policemen in very old khaki uniforms had somebody's suitcase open and was searching it. A police officer was examining the hotel register.

"What goes on?" I asked a British red cap, a corporal, who was smoking in a corner. Plainly, he thought I was drunk. So did I, in a way.

"Somebody jus' threw herself off the Pyramid," he said. "At least, she tried to. They can't get her down. She's stuck up there near the top. Chaps are going up there like some bloody mountain rescue team."

That was how my wedding went. It seemed a wedding at the time. It seems a wedding still. Every time I've passed a car with streamers and a bride in white I've thought, that is how my wedding was. Because there was no ceremony about my night with Nadia I've tried to borrow the trappings of every ceremony

46

I've seen since. At a penitential church in Portugal, I borrowed them, among cypresses and lawns and clipped camellias with a double stone staircase, lined with statues of the saints and marble masks, descending in the hot sunshine for a quarter of a mile the steep side of a hill. By chance I was there, when the couple came out of the church to be photographed. This is my wedding, I thought – oh! it was years later. This is it all right. This is Nadia. This is me. The rite is beyond understanding.

The photographer worked. The family stood back while he posed the bride and groom among the camellias. The groom was in black and inconspicuous. The bride's white veil and dress flowed in the light breeze. She flickered among the trees. The clipped camellias were huge spinning tops, painted over with pink and red blossoms. The bride was Nadia. Up that staircase, towards her, the penitents were supposed to climb on their knees; and as I remember those marble masks, I see now that they were part of an elaborate artificial cascade. The water coursed downhill, through baroque vents and channels. At one level it burst through the mouths of the masks, at the next through the ears, then the nostrils and, in clear jets, from the open eyes. I remember the piteousness of those streaming eyes and how the mask they belonged to had the familiar turnip grin and little white ears standing out on either side.

Not in reality. It was a dream that produced the weeping face of Uncle Raymond somewhere on that penitential staircase; and above it statues of men and angels, all the way up to the church façade propping the blue sky, to the pigeons and flowering trees where the photographer hid under the black cloth of his old-fashioned tripod camera, gesturing to Nadia so that she moved slightly this way, or that, lifting her head or an arm in noontide silence. The mask wept without sound.

That evening I was out in the desert with Major McKellar again, watching him throw the hammer. He had waited for me until about two and then driven back to camp. Now he wanted to know what had detained me. When I said my girl friend had slipped and hurt herself climbing the Great Pyramid in the dark and was now in the Deaconess's Hospital with a broken arm and bruising, he remarked, "A good little hospital that. Run by a German Order of nuns. Knew a Swiss pathologist who was a consultant there. Maybe he still is. I met him on holiday and he told me he had this consultancy. It's the way to make money, you know, prescribing for these Pashas. They've all got something the matter with their guts. He had a bloody great house in Lugano. He showed me photos of it, this Swiss chap."

"She's my aunt," I said.

"Oh aye!"

"She's an Egyptian and she thinks she's the Sphinx."

"Well, now!" He had been pacing out the distance he had thrown his house bricks. Apparently it was no good because he spent some time swearing and scratching his head. He came back to the foot of the dune where I was sitting. "You're a strange laddie. You know that? When I was in the Black Watch do you know what my officer would have said if I'd kept him up till gone two in the morning, and even then not turned up? All right, don't say it. I connived at your behaviour, masquerading as an officer and all, but you seem to take it all as your due! That's what gets me. If I'd had a night on the tiles at least I'd be showing a bit of gratitude. What's this about your aunt? Now why d'you tell me all that?" he said, when I had explained a bit about Nadia. "You must have the Devil in you. Both of you."

I thought about this. "You've got to have a bit of the Devil in you."

"Now what are you on about?"

I was angry with everybody: Nadia, Uncle Raymond, Major McKellar and even Hitler who, to be honest, I hadn't felt about personally until then; for the first time I knew he was a Very Bad Man because I was a damned too – and if the Major swung that improvised hammer over the next dune and in looking for it lost his sense of direction, as he said he would, then I could imagine myself quietly withdrawing. Major McKellar could walk off into the middle of the Sahara for all I cared.

"I don't know," I said.

"It's a funny thing, climbing the Pyramid in the dark."

"She was trying to kill herself."

"Is that what she said?"

She said just that in the taxi on the way back to Cairo. It was the only conveyance I could get. She had a black eye, a grazed cheek, and her left arm strapped up between a couple of box-wood slats taken out of the hotel kitchen. She was in consider-able pain, a bit hysterical, yet this was the time I chose to tell her I loved her; it was just crazy to think of doing some injury to herself. We had been brought together by fate, and so on. I would make her happy.

"Now I know I'm a whore," she shouted. "You would never have made love to me if I'd been married to your uncle. I'm just a concubine and a whore and a bitch. That's my life! That's me!"

"A bloody funny way to do away with yourself." I was heart-less from shock. "It was exhibitionism. What are you going to tell Uncle Raymond?"

"I suppose you'd rather I jumped in the Nile?"

"I don't believe you tried to kill yourself. You're not pinning that sort of guilt on me."

When I told Major McKellar he pulled out a pipe and filled it slowly. There was no wind in the desert that evening, so the flame of his match was steady.

"You've got a problem there, laddie," he said after a few puffs. "She was testing you, in a manner of speaking. She's a Copt, you say. The table of kindred and affinity may be differ-ent from what we have in Scotland. It may be legal to marry your auntie in these parts for all we know. That would be worth looking into. They're all heretics, I wouldn't be surprised. What possessed your uncle to conceal his first marriage from your auntie?"

"He's quirky."

Major McKellar considered this. "Is that all you've got to com-municate? Shall I tell you something? Your aunt is as stiff-necked as he is, but being a foreigner she's going to do a lot of damage before she's finished. You're green to be caught up in so much torment," he said quaintly.

"I love her. I want to marry her." I had spoken brutally to her

49

but I was dazed and besotted. Nadia was everywhere. She came at me from the sky and sand. She encompassed me.

"Look, laddie," said the Major. "What exactly went on in Mena House last night?" I told him, and he thought about it carefully before saying, "It doesn't add up. Somebody is having somebody on."

The unit moved off north to the Wadi Latrun area where there were some monasteries I thought tenderly of because they were Coptic. I couldn't ring Nadia up now. I wrote to her but I can't have a go at re-creating the kind of rubbish I must have written. We had no mail for three weeks. The C.O. was making experiments to see how long we could last without water. Major Mc-Kellar had the job of analysing everybody's urine. There were Bedouin in this area and I had no conscience about slipping behind a dune and accepting a swig of foul water. Eventually a jeep came back from Alexandria with a bag of mail and sure enough there was a letter for me with a Cairo postmark. There was mail from home too, but that did not seem important. I went off some mile and a half to the shade of a monastery wall to read this letter. As follows, roughly.

Dear Sir,
Professor Foulkes has been in correspondence and informs me about you. So I take the presumption to write at your military address and say I am the father of Nadia who is enjoying holidays with her cousins in Minia and I would be happy to welcome you. Sir, you are the nephew of your uncle. I am the father of the bride of your uncle. Also, I have a son, Kamil, who teaches school in Assiut where doubtless Nadia will visit with him because Minia and Assiut are not remote, each from the other. Your auntie has been suffering but she is established again and rejoicing and breathing the pure air of Upper Egypt, which is the cradle of my people.
If you will be in Cairo, my dear sir and kinsman, you will call on me. It will be an honour and my house may be yours and everything although my wife was dying these some years

ago. I am a widower, Mr. Cozens. Now that the Germans attack Russia they cannot attack Egypt and I am quite sure all soldiers have leave. Egypt is a hospitable country where our Lord and Saviour was finding a safe lair as an infant in the Famous Flight as depicted by the Great Artists. So make haste to telephone me or write. Do not delay, my dear boy.

Ibr. Guirgis, Avocat-Notaire.

Re-creating the letter brings back the glare of the desert, the cool shade of the monastery wall and the man himself, Dr. Guirgis, graduate of the Faculty of Law, Fouad el Awal University; and the questions bubble up. Why did Nadia not write when her father did? Why had she gone to Minia? Was the man I hit in the mouth really her father? Was he Ibr. Guirgis? What was Ibr.?

After that night in Mena House I was like some addict cut off from his drug. Nadia might be crazy but so what? We'd run off together. We'd go to the Congo. We'd live with the pygmies in the rain forests. If Nadia hated and despised her father that was O.K. by me, and I would hate and despise him too. But, in her absence I had to see him. Nadia stayed on in Upper Egypt. That letter from Ibr. Guirgis I just carried about with me; and I took it out and read it from time to time.

When at last we met, and he turned out to be indeed the man I had hit in the mouth, he didn't recognise me. He had no idea I and the soldier who had knocked him down were one and the same. As I have said, it was a dark staircase.

"Mr. Cozens," he said, "never forget that every human being is the same as every other human being. All! English, Egyptian, Christian, Moslem, all the same beneath the skin. It is treason to the human race not to know we are all the same beneath the skin. That is why Shakespeare's Shylock and Othello are English. They are English, both. Why not, dear Cozens? What follows? We believe! On the other hand, we do not believe in Pierre Loti's foreigners. We do *not* believe in Somerset Maugham's foreigners. We do *not* believe in Conrad's Indonesians, or Forster's Indians or Lawrence's Mexicans. They are all strange for-

51

eigners. Wogs. There are no wogs in Shakespeare. Wogs have been in literature since Fenimore Cooper invented Red Indians. Queer, *other* people, I am a wog to you, Cozens! But I am not to another person. I am not strange. Your aunt is not strange. I am the same as you. Wogs are people."

He was a bookish old bird and "bird" is the right metaphor because it conveys his delicacy and quickness. He had new, rather ill-fitting, dentures which were the most robust part of his features. His lips seemed pouched to contain them and when he smiled the large, even, white dentures provided more brilliance than could possibly have been intended. Steel-rimmed spectacles made him look a bit owlish. On his head he wore a little red felt cap wound round with several yards of white cotton.

"I don't think you're a wog," I said.

"Then you are a remarkable young man," he said, staring at me curiously. "And confident. You must not deceive yourself. It is difficult to understand and deal faithfully with people of a different race. It is *much* easier to write them off as mysterious and unpredictable. I come back to Shakespeare. He didn't make Othello inscrutable. It reminds me, a bit, of what Mr. Eliot said about landscape in connection with Thomas Hardy. Hardy used landscape to project his own fantasies. You mustn't use *foreignness* to project yours. There is no such thing as foreigner, Cozens. Be a realist. Avoid fantasy. To me, you are a Copt, as I am."

"I don't see that at all."

Now I see it sufficiently well to want to set down Guirgis's conversation not as it actually was (the letter gives a fair sample) but what it would have been if English had been his mother tongue. It takes away the quaintness; the real Guirgis was not quaint. It is the kind of justice he would expect; he was warning me not to pop him into the funny foreigner category. So here is Guirgis plain. Justice to the past is, after all, what this writing is supposed to establish.

He had an old stone house in a village. Because the house and the village were in a grove of date palms the first impression was of coolness and shade. Only afterwards did you realise the villagers were living in reeking mud hovels, together with their chickens and goats. Flies gathered about the eyes and mouths of the children. A couple of lead buffaloes wallowed clumsily in a pond. The only pleasant smell was a bitter one that made the eyes tingle; dried camel dung being burned, I was told, in the bread ovens. But Guirgis's house was a contrast. He said it was over two hundred years old, built with stone raided from some ancient burial area on the edge of the desert, and in what he called the Maghreb style. A lot of people came from the west, from Morocco and Tunis a couple of hundred or more years ago and built houses like this. Instead of an ordinary ceiling in the main room it had a dome going up to a height of thirty feet or so.

There was no evidence of Nadia's having been there. Guirgis said this was his summer house. Most of the year he and his family had lived in a flat in Cairo. Now he was alone he still kept the two places on.

I still didn't know what I could take for granted and what I couldn't. Egypt had put me into a spin. Nadia had provided an almighty acceleration. What was normal? Perhaps it was not all that uncommon to fall in love with one's aunt. If Nadia was crazy perhaps there were lots of women crazy in the same way. Only experience would tell and the world promised more experience than I could bear. As for Guirgis, sitting opposite me and drinking some kind of herb tea, perhaps he was only one of a whole tribe of apparently intelligent and restrained old chaps who were given to sudden attacks on strangers. It didn't seem likely but I wasn't sure. Did he smoke hashish? I didn't like sitting there knowing he had attacked me and that he was ignorant of the fact. He might even attack me again.

"You have met your aunt. Now, what do you think of her? She has had this little accident since seeing you, not serious and is recuperating with her cousin. She is typically English, is she not? Well, not typically. Perhaps that is to exaggerate. In the family we think of her as the English one. She is composed and well disciplined. When you met her I am sure you did not think she was a foreign lady. This is my experience. When I meet English and French and Italians and Greeks I do not think of them as foreign ladies and gentlemen. They are people like me. My son-in-law is a most unusual man. Professor Foulkes is unusual because he is Professor Foulkes, not because he is an Englishman. You are aware, Mr. Cozens, that there is not complete accord between your aunt and your uncle?"

"He's been ill." I couldn't think what to say. How much did Guirgis know? "What's this little accident she's had?" I wanted his version but he brushed my question aside.

"It is his second marriage. It was wrong of Professor Foulkes not to tell me that he was married before. It has caused trouble."

"Like this accident?"

"Your aunt Nadia's confidence was destroyed. Naturally. I believe Professor Foulkes when he says he divorced his first wife. He has sent to England for the document which will prove it. It will come. But in war it takes a long time. I believe him. Nadia does not. Now, you must know the truth about his first marriage."

"I don't know whether he was divorced, if that's what you mean. I was too young."

"You do not know?" Guirgis looked at me through his big steel-rimmed glasses. He seemed incredulous. "But such things would be spoken of in the family."

"I didn't know."

"Do you believe he divorced his first wife?"

"I don't know."

"But he *must* have divorced her. Either he divorced her or he killed her. There is no alternative. Absolutely not, with a man like that. What was the name of your first aunt?"

"Treasure."

"Professor Foulkes did not kill her?"

"Kill her?" He had put the question in such a matter-of-fact way. "No, he must have divorced her. I cannot understand why Nadia is so unhappy about it all. He ought to have told her," I said. "I mean, about being married before."

"I asked him and he even denied he had been married before."

"He doesn't like answering questions."

"Dear Mr. Cozens, I live just to reconcile your aunt and your uncle. My life now has no other purpose. Will you do what you can to help me in this?"

"I'm in the Army. There's this war."

"When you see your aunt next you must tell her she must cherish her husband and receive him. She must change. She must believe him. She is a Christian wife."

"Even if she'd listen to me," I said, "I couldn't talk to her like that."

"Why not?"

"I just couldn't, that's all."

"When they are reunited and I see my grandchild I shall die happy."

This sounded horrible to me. "If Uncle Raymond had killed Aunt Treasure they'd have hanged him."

"Not in Egypt. Laws are different but human nature is the same. In your uncle's position I would have got Aunt Treasure to Egypt and killed her here. I understand your uncle. Are we not both men?"

He was such a tiny man I thought that if it came to a straight fight Aunt Treasure would have probably done away with him with ease.

Later in the afternoon we went for a walk, out of the grove of palm trees. We stood on a baked track in the middle of a meadow of what looked like lucerne and the roasting heat seemed to come up from the ground. The country rolled away from us. Guirgis explained that we were in a depression, the Fayyoum oasis, which was like nowhere else in Egypt. That village over there was So-and-so of the Apricots. Beyond, was So-and-so of the Figs. All the villages had names that linked them with the fruits they best grew. But he was mainly interested in the fact that the Allies had, after a bit of fighting, taken over Syria and Lebanon. The fighting had been with the Vichy French. This was a grief to everyone like himself who admired French culture but it was a cruel war, it had been justifiable for the British to cripple the French fleet at Oran and Mers-el-Kebir in the July of the previous year. And the good thing about the liberation of Syria and Lebanon was that the fine horses of those countries would now be able to come down for the Egyptian racing season.

"Racing?"

"Surely. There is a fine course on Gezireh, another at Heliopolis and another at Alexandria. Before the war the greatest jockeys of Europe came. And Australia. The Syrians have excellent horses. Mr. Cozens, when the season starts we will go to the Heliopolis races and bet heavily on Syrian horses. It is only common sense that if an owner sends a horse all the way from Syria he believes it has a good chance of winning. No doubt you are always at Newmarket and such places? I have never been in England. Auteuil I am fond of. It is a good course. When I was a young man I won a lot of money at Auteuil."

"You wouldn't kill a woman, really, would you?" I said. "Uncle Raymond wouldn't."

"If my honour as a man were touched. Yes, I would kill a woman. So would Professor Foulkes. You are young. In the army you must have killed men."

"I'm in the Medical Corps."

"You are a soldier of conscience? An objector to killing?"

"No, I'd like to get into a combatant unit."

"I shall speak to General Auchinleck. He is an intimate friend of mine and often in my box at the Sporting Club. If you go into a combatant unit you will help me with your aunt? It might be you became an officer. Why are you not an officer? It is absurd. If I persuade the General to give you a commission in a fighting unit you will speak to your Aunt Nadia about her life. I am desperate, Mr. Cozens. I really am *desperate*."

Before he dropped me in the Midan Ismailia I asked him again about Nadia's accident. "She had a little slip while climbing a pyramid. I don't know which one. Young people sometimes climb pyramids in the dark to see the dawn. It is a way of making continuity with their ancestors. Just a broken collar-bone and a greenstick fracture of the humerus. A lot of bad bruising. She was blue and black. I trust you enjoyed this trip into the country. You are posted in Cairo again now, so we must arrange such another excursion. You shall come racing with me."

Guirgis went racing as other men went on a binge. After laying his bets he walked about in a kind of trance. When the horses came round the bend for the final straight he was corpse-like with excitement. A loss to Guirgis was something he brushed aside. To be with him when he won was to see, in his fragile body, the ecstasy of lust triumphant. He scarcely knew where he was or who he was. He ceased to be Guirgis. His colour went. He shouted and waved his skinny hands, as though the god of gambling himself had taken possession.

He was right about my being back in Cairo. I had been posted back from the L.R.D.G. and told to get shaved. Colonel Patch was good enough to tell me why. The L.R.D.G. were an élite group and the C.O. of my unit thought I was not élite enough. I didn't seem reliable. I was brittle and he wanted tougher-minded chaps about him. Major McKellar and I kept in touch, though. The unit returned to near the Pyramids and he came into Cairo from time to time and lent me one of his old shirts with pips on so that we could go into Shepheard's together. We had an arrangement whereby if I was caught I'd say I'd pinched it. And I was bound to be caught. In a way it was what I now wanted. Nadia did not answer my letters and stayed in Upper Egypt. If I was court-martialled I could say it was all because I wasn't in a fighting unit. I was brittle all right, suicidal was a better way of putting it. You never knew but that would do the trick. Uncle Raymond wrote to say he was getting stronger every day. From Nadia not a word.

On some occasion Uncle Raymond said, "We've got to remember we're living through a drama. Everyone knows we're on the eve of a battle, and in years to come you'll show your scars and say they were wounds you had in action, though naturally I hope you don't have so much as a scratch. But think of the yarning."

"This is different."

"You'll see old age, Tishy."

"I don't feel I'm living in a drama, that's all."

"Life only appears to be open and neutral," he said. "We have to live with the thought of what our memories will be. St. Antony's thoughts were entirely teleological, that goes without saying. Alexander the Great, we are told, deliberately lived a life based on the pattern of a Homeric hero."

"What's teleological?"

"He knew there was a story moving to an end and to some purpose, did St. Antony. I shall look back and you will look back. Old men forget; yet all shall be forgot but you'll remember with advantages – that means exaggeration," he added, always the teacher.

"There's been nothing like how we are now. There's no story."

"I believe," said Uncle Raymond, "that there *is* a story and to be really human is to discern it."

At the time I didn't realise he was quoting *Henry V* and couldn't in any case have guessed the possible advantages that tug and have to be resisted. But story? What did he mean by that? Story?

chapteR 4

 An evening in early August I was coming out of the main bar in Shepheard's and cutting through that dark Moorish lounge with its lattice-work screens, ornate chairs and tables, looking agreeably ornate myself; new, well-polished brown shoes, officer style, khaki stockings with a red thread to show where you turned them down, brown shorts I'd bought from a South African, a new bush shirt over and outside these shorts and, of course, the three cloth pips Mc-Kellar had lent me on each shoulder. Except for the pips the kit is the same as I'm wearing at this minute. So far as I remember that evening in Shepheard's was the first time I had assembled the outfit. Anything went those days provided it looked even vaguely military. I had a fly whisk like a horse's tail for touching my flat cap – McKellar's too – and acknowledging salutes. Where did the fly whisk go? Perhaps back to McKellar. An officer got up from his chair as I passed and said, "Hey, Tishy!"

It was Uncle Raymond, and he was a major now. He had new cloth crowns up. His illness had aged him. There were deep lines from his nostrils to the corners of his mouth where his big yellow teeth forced the lips apart. He was beginning to look an old yokel. The short, fat stalks that held his ears appeared to have grown to compensate for the flesh he had lost elsewhere, from his cheeks which had become just a little hollow, and from his throat which was scrawny. Like a bald man who grows a beard, so Uncle Raymond's residual vitality had pushed his ears out and away from his head. Or had he, when I saw him last, worn his

59

hair longer? His appearance jolted me in more ways than one. He raised a hand and it was positively skinny.

"Tishy! It is Tishy, isn't it? What are you got up like that for? I wrote you a letter only this afternoon. I wanted to tell you my good news. Everything is all right, Tishy. But you've got pips up! What's the game?" He was ducking his head from side to side as he talked, or hissed rather, his eyes everywhere. "If you're *spotted*, Tishy?"

"You know I don't like being called that, Uncle Raymond."

"You're dressed as an officer."

"Can't get in here unless you are. What do you mean, though, everything is all right?"

"Your aunt and I. We're together again. As you know, there was this misunderstanding. But it's all cleared up. She had a nasty fall and was laid up. Gave her time to think, I suppose. But she's perfectly all right. It's like it used to be. Tishy, for God's sake come with me to the lavatory and take those pips off. We'll go to the Y.M.C.A. Oh, dammit, I can't do that, though. I'm meeting the Padre."

At that moment a grey-headed man in very correct, well-pressed tropical kit – slacks, not shorts, brightly polished metal crowns on his shoulders, a dog collar and purple shirt-front – came up and shook hands with Uncle Raymond, saying he was sorry to be late but –

"This is my nephew, Captain Cozens," said Uncle Raymond. He introduced the chaplain as Ronnie Penhaligon. "He's only been out here a few months. Major Penhaligon," he explained to me, "used to be chaplain to the Anglican Bishop in Jerusalem. So we've been friends since before the war."

"What's your first name, captain?" said Penhaligon in a steely, American way that puzzled me for a moment. "Mine's Ronnie. Nice to meet you, Dave. Why don't we just go off and have a nice co-o-o-l drink? Your uncle and I met up in Petra. We were there with this missionary. Do you remember that, Raymond? He looked round at those rock carvings and marvellous temples and do you remember? He said no doubt it was a fine city in its time but we had to remember it was built by the heathen." Penhaligon laughed noisily.

He was steering us back towards the bar as he talked. I was keeping an eye cocked for McKellar because he was due to arrive at any moment. Too much was happening at once. He'd twig immediately the auntie I'd told him about was Uncle Raymond's wife.

"What a good thing this war is!" said Penhaligon when finally he had us seated at a big brass-topped table. "Bad in some ways. Let us not deceive ourselves. War is a bad thing. But what is fine, Dave, is that you are a young lad and you know you are fighting for good against evil. I'm an American but I have the honour to hold a commission from His Gracious Majesty, King George VI against the day my own country enters the war. It is a source of great satisfaction to me that the issues are clear cut in the way they are. No ambiguity. Hitler is the devil incarnate and the Germans are evil in this generation. So there are no problems. Life is easy. We shall fight and we shall win. But if we are defeated we shall know we have died for the right." While he was making this speech he held his brimming glass so close to his mouth I thought he would be taking a swig at any moment. But he didn't. "I'll be honest with you. If my country comes in I'll have to consider my position because do you know what? I'd get *three times* as much pay as a padre in the United States army! Of course, I'd still be on the same side."

"I don't see it clear cut," I said. "Nothing is clear cut."

"You sound like a fifth columnist to me," said Penhaligon.

"Tishy is only saying he doesn't want to be taken in by propaganda, aren't you, Tishy?" Before he could be interrupted, Uncle Raymond went on hurriedly, "There are lots of Anglicans in the United States and Ronnie here is just one of them, if you should be wondering. It would not surprise me in the slightest if one day the Archbishop of Canterbury was an American. I'm not sure about the constitutional position. You can't have the monarch crowned by a foreigner, very well, could you, so I suppose they would have to disestablish the Church."

If I were to give Penhaligon's glass a bob the beer would go all over his purple shirt front because he still hadn't taken a sip of the stuff. He was holding the glass up to his face and staring at me with what I judged to be hostility. But I did not bob his glass. "I'm not a fifth colmunist."

"You don't really see any good in Hitler, do you?" Penhaligon demanded.

"He's a man. He must have his points."

"Hitler has no points! He is just evil. He is supported by men who are just evil. Don't you believe there is such a thing as evil?"

"I don't believe in evil I'm not capable of myself."

"Aw, crap!"

Uncle Raymond was trying to break this up by talking about the constitutional position raised by a New Zealand, Australian or even Indian, Archbishop of Canterbury but Penhaligon seemed quite maddened by this talk of evil. He stuck out a heavy jaw and said thickly, "Don't give me that, you little turd! Not believe in the existence of any evil you're not capable of yourself! What arrogance! What false pride! You're not the measure of God's creation. Be humble, I tell you this. We're fighting on the side of virtue and civilisation against Hell itself."

"You're no better than anybody else."

"Look here, Ray," said Penhaligon, "I didn't come here to be talked to like this."

"All the hell is not over there, that's all," I said. "We could make hell. All of us. I could." It was true. I could feel the devil rise inside me as I talked, I could do for this Penhaligon. I could do for Uncle Raymond too, particularly Uncle Raymond, now that he and Nadia were together again.

"Oh, come, Tishy. You haven't even read *Mein Kampf*, I'm sure."

"I don't need to read a book to know what I'm capable of."

"Because you're a nasty little brute," said Penhaligon, changing his ground, "you must not think everybody else is a nasty brute too."

"Shall I tell you something? That's just what I do think."

It was time for the military police picquet to make its routine inspection. Their main job was collecting drunks and I had been sufficiently accustomed to the Shepheard's routine to know that it was normally limited to a quick inspection by a C.M.P. officer, just checking to see whether any officer was high and talking too much or whether there was a spy or two to be picked up; but tonight they gave Shepheard's the full treatment, such as they might have given to the Y.M.C.A. beer garden in Soleiman Pasha and the whole picquet with steel hats and sidearms came clumping through: an Army Military Policeman, a Navy M.P. in white pants and leggings, an Australian, a New Zealander, a South African and a Gurkha. If I was to be taken in for being improperly dressed, in that I, a private, presented himself in the style and badges of a commissioned officer, this was as good a time as any; and I was all prepared for arrest because Padre Ronnie Penhaligon was obviously itching to call one of these policemen over and say I'd been talking sedition. He did not do so immediately, out of respect for Uncle Raymond, no doubt.

"Don't let's kid ourselves," I said to Penhaligon, having drunk my beer – it was the fourth that evening and I wasn't really used to the stuff – and put my face close enough for him to smell my breath. "We're all in this. It isn't just the Nazis who are black and damned, and when we're fighting them we're fighting ourselves in a way. Do you understand that? 'Course you bloody don't! You're too pleased with yourself. The Nazi army is full of buggers like you."

"Shut up!" Uncle Raymond snapped this out in a way that made me jump. "He's my nephew. A bit hysterical, and drunk. Bad news, you know." He said this to the officer in charge of the picquet who had come over to see what was going on. I could see by his armband that he was the Assistant Provost Marshal himself. "I'll take him home. I live here. He's on leave."

"He was talking treason," said Penhaligon with relish.

"Not at all. Let's get this straight." We were all standing up, the picquet more or less round us and I was conscious that the rest of the people in the bar were not taking a blind bit of notice. They were drinking and laughing and talking, just as though life was going on normally when in fact, in their midst, it had been given a sort of wrench and twist. I really did feel I'd been granted some profound moral insight and I just wanted to express it for the benefit of all. Not only my life would be altered, but theirs too. After an illumination of this kind nobody could go on in the same old way. I was so excited I saw the course of the war being changed. Nobody, absolutely nobody, had seen what I had seen.

"Let's get this straight. I was saying nobody's better than anybody else." Put in that way I had to admit my insight didn't sound so profound after all and I could see it was not having much effect on the Assistant Provost Marshal, nor the Aussie standing on his right, nor for that matter, even the Gurkha who stood on his left and probably had that blank expression on his face at the best of times. I had to admit that what I said sounded silly. But it did not persuade me the illumination was anything but real and irreversible. Understandably, I was inarticulate about it. I was not going to find words to persuade these chaps. But life was going to be different. By God! it was and let everybody look out!

"Captain Cozens said we were as bad as the Nazis." Penhaligon squeezed this out. "Sorry about this, Ray, but the truth's got to come out. It's the kindest thing in the long run."

Uncle Raymond looked wretched and, although I hated him because of what he had said about Nadia, I couldn't help feeling a bit sorry. After all, he had been ill and now he was bewildered by the turn things had taken. "We were talking about the Archbishop of Canterbury," he explained to the Assistant Provost Marshal, "and the conversation naturally turned in a theological direction. The Padre was expressing a view of the war which my nephew misunderstood to be Manichaean. You know what that is?"

"No," said the Assistant Provost Marshal, "but it sounds interesting."

"The ancient doctrine that pure good and pure evil are in conflict in the universe."

"I didn't say that, Ray. My theology is real copper-bottomed."

"It was implicit in your view, Ronnie. And in so far as you were saying the Nazis stood for the forces of darkness and evil and the Allies stood for light and goodness I must say I thought young Tishy was perfectly right to take you up and put the orthodox Christian view, which is that good and evil are much more mixed up than that. I'm sorry, Ronnie." He sounded absolutely furious with Ronnie, actually.

"I'm not a fucking heretic," said Penhaligon.

I was annoyed with Uncle Raymond for implying that my unique and unprecedented insight into the forces of human nature had been anticipated by Christianity (*orthodox* too, which made it even more slighting). I reckoned you could not get more orthodox and conventional than Ronnie Penhaligon and if he didn't know how smug he was who in Christendom did? He didn't seem to know too much about good and evil being mixed up.

"No, what I'm saying is worse than that," I said to Uncle Raymond. "I don't believe *anyone* is any good, really, at bottom."

"In real life," said Uncle Raymond to the Assistant Provost Marshal, "I'm Professor Foulkes. My nephew was at Dunkirk."

"Calais," I put in.

"Time we were making for home, Tishy." He slapped me on the back, laughed himself in a metallic sort of way and obviously hoped everyone else would laugh too. "Your aunt will be expecting us."

The Assistant Provost Marshal gave the impression that, firstly, he was not at home in theology; and secondly, when he looked at Ronnie Penhaligon, that he wondered why the United States was so slow in coming into the war. "Professor, I'll be back in this bar in ten minutes and if you're not out of it with this officer by that time –" he meant me – "I'll be asking to see the documents of all concerned. That goes for you too, Padre."

"Are you asking me to leave the hotel?" said Penhaligon stiffly. "I've made a serious charge against this officer."

"No. It's Captain –" He looked at me interrogatively.

"Cozens," I said.

Major Penhaligon actually stood to attention and the Assistant Provost Marshal with his picquet clattered away to where I imagined the management had drinks set up for them.

McKellar, whom I had not noticed before, now stepped forward, clapped his hands on both my shoulders and said, "I threw it sixty-five feet, three and a half inches this afternoon, David, which is a long way less than I'm capable of. But it's better than when you were supervising. Now, who are these gentlemen? Do we know each other? I have to inform you, young David, I saw you in conversation with the constabulary. Who's for belly dancing?"

"I'm just drinking tonight," I said.

"Are you for belly dancing, Padre? I thought the Runners had got young David here by the short and curly, didn't you? A real relief to see them bugger off. But sixty-five feet, three and a half inches! I suppose that sounds nothing to you, Padre, but you can't get a grip of the bloody thing. The handle's just wire. What's everyone drinking?"

Uncle Raymond stepped forward and said he was Major Foulkes of the Canal Defence Force, my uncle, and he was taking me home. He also introduced Major Penhaligon and McKellar said, "So you're married to the boy's auntie, are you? Well, now, I'm that interested to meet you."

"I'm not going with you," I said to Uncle Raymond.

"Yes, you are, Tishy." He seized my upper arm in an unexpectedly vice-like grip and began pushing me through the crowd. He was really hurting me. I had no idea he was so strong.

" 'Night, Ronnie," he said. " 'Night, major."

Penhaligon and McKellar looked after us, Penhaligon like a frustrated tiger and McKellar clearly hurt that his convivial evening had been messed up – because the Padre seemed not to be coming to the belly dancing with him – but anxious to retrieve something from the wreckage. I saw him take Penhaligon by the arm, wave in our direction, frown, begin muttering and obviously preparing himself to be as indiscreet as hell.

There were no taxis, so I remember bowling along with Uncle Raymond in the back of one of those horse-drawn open gharries, the bright lights of the city wobbling and rocking out of the spongy night and the tarbooshed driver unnecessarily cracking his whip and shouting from time to time. One moment I wanted to jump out and run; for the most part I was just aching to see Nadia and it was no good deceiving myself. Uncle Raymond unbuttoned the flaps on my shoulders, removed the cloth stars and put them in his pocket.

"You're a young fool. Thank God I happened to turn up. You'd have had six months in the glass house. Do you know what that could do to you? That military prison at Abbassia is a sadist's delight. They'd kill you. What your poor mother would say, I don't know." And so on. He couldn't see the joke at all. "As for that Medical Corps major you introduced me to, he looks a complete idiot. If he's been aiding and abetting you I've a good mind to report the matter. You really must promise me, Tishy, you'll never do anything so foolish again."

"How long has Nadia been back from Minia?"

"Aren't you listening? You just seem to want to destroy yourself."

When we reached the flat Uncle Raymond could not, to begin with, find Nadia and walked about the place – not that it was all that large – shouting for her as though we were out in the forest and she was hiding behind a tree. "Tishy's here, darling. Where are you, sweetie?" He did not seem aware this was an odd way to behave and it gave me the comforting impression Nadia regularly hid away from him. In spite of what Uncle Raymond had said I didn't believe they were sleeping together again. She wouldn't have agreed to that. It would have been too disgusting.

She had been taking a bath and now emerged wearing nothing, so far as I could judge, but slippers consisting of a flat board and red toe-cap, and a silky custard-yellow dressing-gown with huge, floppy sleeves. This gown was moulded closely to her body and secured by a broad, loosely knotted sash. The neck was very full, almost cut square so that her full, tight white breasts were revealed almost to the nipples. Her hair piled up on top of her head and secured with a comb, was black with a lot of blue in

67

it because it was vapour moist. The effect was foreign and strange; I thought of her father's warning against using the exotic to project personal fantasies. But it would have been impossible to look at that broad face and full lips without feeling there was an erotic force we didn't know about at home; or, to be more exact, I in my green shirt did not know about. She looked back as though she had never seen me in her life before. It was the first time we had met for two months.

"What are you doing here?" she demanded of Uncle Raymond. "I thought you were out for the evening. It really is not right to come back without warning, bringing someone. You have no idea what I might have been doing."

"How's your arm?" I asked.

She started ticking Uncle Raymond off again but she changed her mind and looked at me with her head slightly on one side and her throat seemed long and vulnerable, almost swan-like.

"I heard you had a fall and broke your arm," I said. "How is it?"

"Perfectly all right," she said after she had stared at me for some moments in silence. "How did you know I broke my arm?"

"For one thing," I said, "I came to see you in hospital. You tried to kill yourself. Remember?"

"I didn't know you'd visited Nadia in hospital," said Uncle Raymond.

"There's a lot you don't know."

"It was very thoughful of you. Wasn't it, Nadia? How very nice."

Nadia laughed. "It was a little secret."

Uncle Raymond brushed all this aside. "I'm really very cross with Tishy because he's been foolish and I rescued him only in the nick of time. There are no secrets between us, Nadia. I have to tell you he was dressed as an officer. This information must not go outside this room. Tishy could be court-martialled."

Nadia went off to dress and Uncle Raymond paced up and down lecturing me about the need to obey rules in general and King's Regulations in particular because they were based not on a theory of inequality as between one man and another but simply so that everyone knew what to do in particular circumstances. He'd been young himself. He knew what it was to be impatient. But until the war was over everything was subordinate to the needs of victory. Nothing else mattered – personal status, neuroses, ambition, selfishness, all the greeds and passions of the individual which, in peace time, had opportunities to flower, all these were now subject to the exigencies of military service. He said he did not live up to this standard himself. He was ashamed of the way he had broken down when Nadia had failed to visit him in hospital. But she didn't like the hospital smells. I had been right to tell the Padre all men were capable of sin. The fact remained that there was a clear-cut moral issue in the war and we had to put our backs into winning it. We must not fool about pretending to be officers if we were not.

"I don't believe places should be Officers Only."

"Don't shout, Tishy. Remember, I'm your uncle. What I'm telling you is for your good."

Nadia now came back dressed more conventionally (though she was still naked in my eyes, and, wherever she was in the room, apparently close to me and touching me with soft firm limbs and breasts – a real example of the erotic and exotic projecting personal fantasies!); she was in a long, cool, grey dress and she had let her hair down; it was loose and it seemed to touch my lips every time I looked at it. She knew all this. But she put on a great act about how unfair it was to bring guests home without warning; there was no food in the house and no servant to cook it even if there was. She had been intending to make a simple supper for herself of cold chicken, cheese and yoghourt, but there really was not enough to go round.

"I'm not staying. Don't worry about me," I said.

"Where are you going?" She spoke contemptuously, as though I knew perfectly well she had this spell or curse upon me; I simply was not free to come or go, except at her bidding. Major McKellar's remark when I told him what had happened at Mena House came into my mind. "It doesn't add up. Somebody is having somebody on." Here she was, behaving like a petulant suburban housewife when she didn't give a damn, really, about food and unexpected guest, and the rest. Underneath she was the girl who had been outraged to discover Uncle Raymond had been married before, had laughed to see her father knocked down, made love with me and tried – or so she claimed – to kill herself. My argument with Ronnie Penhaligon had given me such a feeling of the diabolical I wanted to shout all this out for Uncle Raymond's benefit. You bloody cuckold! I wanted to say.

"Where all the other troops go on a night off," I said as though I'd been giving her question serious consideration. "Round to the red light district."

"To the brothel, you mean?"

She really was standing close to me now and when I nodded in a savage sort of way she was able, without moving a step, to lift her hand and slap my face. There was such force behind the blow I didn't immediately realise what had happened. I just felt tired and shocked. She must have had a ring on that hand because when I put my hand up to my cheek it was bleeding, and it would have needed a ring or something hard like a ring to break the skin.

"Tishy, you shouldn't be so vulgar. Of course, he's not going to the red light district. He's just trying to shock you, Nadia. He's a good boy and you've got to remember he's been through the French campaign. But it was horrible of you to use such language to your aunt, Tishy. Apologise, I insist!"

"I've got nothing to apologise for."

I made for the door and he followed me out on to the landing, talking as he came about the whole thing being his fault at bottom, because of the distrust brought about by his failure to tell Nadia that he had been married, and divorced; and this had upset her because she was a sensible girl, and she had been driven – by his pride and selfishness – to behave foolishly; all that unhappiness was behind them now, thank God! but the last few months had taken their toll. It was only because Nadia was not quite herself that she had struck me. At the same time, my own responsibility for her behaviour must be acknowledged. He feared I was getting into bad company. It was very rude to mention the red light district to respectable Coptic ladies. I didn't really go to brothels, did I? He could believe anything of that Major McKellar, though.

"Let me take a word of apology back to your aunt," said Uncle Raymond, as we stood at the wide doorless entrance hall to 5, Midan Ismailia, under the eye of a fat, unshaven porter who sat at his little wooden table drinking tea out of a tumbler. The trams clashed by, screaming round the sharp bend into Bab el-Louk and giving out tinny flashes of electricity that turned the night sky intermittently mauve and made the buildings away in the distance, pallid and insubstantial like stage scenery.

"I'm not apologising. She's a bitch." I put my hand up to my cheek and one finger came away red.

"Oh, dear," said Uncle Raymond. "I did so want you and Nadia to be friends."

The possibility can be conceded Nadia took me as a lover out of a sense of outraged chastity. I wouldn't have admitted at the time I was merely the instrument at hand. Almost immediately, of course, I became – to Nadia – something else. Instruments are always turning into something else, as Moses' staff turned into a serpent. She was cornered by the serpent and tried to escape. *Of course* she loved me; anybody's first impulse under the shock of real love is to escape.

Some time later Major McKellar reported on what happened after Uncle Raymond and I left him and Ronnie Penhaligon in Shepheard's. Apparently they talked about ice curling. Penhaligon was interested in this. All the stones used in curling clubs in the States were Scottish granite. They curled Scottish granite and drank Scotch whisky in these clubs.

"He thought you needed taking in hand, though. Said you were young and ethically ambivalent. You're not a Nazi, are you, Cozens? No, I was sure you wouldn't be. Major Penhaligon is against the Nazis it seemed to me. He wanted to put them all in concentration camps and experiment on them for medical purposes. However –" and he brightened up at the thought – "I got him along to El-Hati's, and he'd have been out there belly dancing himself if I hadn't begged him to remember his cloth."

Remember, this was before we knew what went on in concentration camps.

In the Cairo Museum I could see Nadia's face carved and painted over and over again. Others may not have seen much of a resemblance but I had only to see the stone face of a goddess for it to flicker and move.

Before going back to the Canal Zone Uncle Raymond introduced me to the Museum because, as he said, he wanted me to see objects that would put current happenings into perspective. In the Mummy Room we inspected long-dead Pharaohs.

"At what point," he asked, "does a human being become an object? One year after death? Or a hundred? A thousand? After three thousand years Ramesses here is a fossil prised from the rock so far as all these sightseers are concerned. What was flesh is now mineral. It just reminds us the Universe didn't *need* to produce life – it could have stayed a waste of gas and flame and crystal. I hope you don't think this is too teleological. There are times, Tishy –"

"For God's sake, don't call me that."

"There are times when I get little flashes of intelligence and I seem to understand why we are and what we are. Do you ever get them, Tishy? Then the moment passes and I don't understand anything any more at all. You are young and you are upset by the evidence of evil in the world. I was most interested in what you were saying to Ronnie Penhaligon. But what is the alternative to life? Rocks and elements and forces! Then I have these flashes. The Universe doesn't seem hostile any more because we *are* the Universe. We are the Universe deciding not to be just physics and chemistry. There was no necessity for it to be anything else. But *it is!* Do you see what I'm getting at?"

"No."

"Neither do I really, but there's this feeling of just teetering on the edge of illumination." After a time spent in examining the Goddess Nut so carved into the underside of a sarcophagus lid that she had to be viewed through a mirror, he went on, "If

I get killed in this war I really do protest. After all, I feel I'm entitled to know *something!* Ah, it's not so unlikely I'll get killed. We're being trained to clear minefields."

What I could have said and didn't was that he had just proved my point about the Nazis having no monopoly of evil. The knowledge he was to clear minefields provided a really evil thrill. I'd be grieved if he got killed but I wanted him dead. Did Nadia? I wondered.

The Goddess Nut was disturbingly like her. You looked down into the mirror to see the reflection of a three-quarter life size bas-relief of the Goddess, with her hands stretched above her head, showing the palms. She had the same firm little breasts as Nadia, the same wide face and full lips, the same snooty smile. The only difference was the way her hair was dressed. The Goddess had firmly braided tresses that seemed to run straight across the forehead and then down on either side of the face, leaving the small ears exposed, to a point about three inches above those firm breasts. She seemed to be on tiptoe. One of the Museum staff, Dr. Ashmuni, told me who she was, that she dated from the 21st Dynasty, was carved out of sandstone and her attitude was one of joy, welcome and protection.

"Protection who for?" I asked.

"The dead," said Dr. Ashmuni, in his melancholy way. Only after many visits to the Museum did I run into Dr. Ashmuni. He was an Egyptologist who had trained in Germany and had a little office of his own where he worked classifying pots. He took me there when, looking up from the mirror where I had been looking at Nut's reflection, I found him watching me with an amused expression on his face. Subsequently he told me I had looked quite alarmed.

"Dr. Ashmuni," I said to him one evening when the museum was shut and he had asked me to stay behind and drink coffee with him in his office. The *farragi* (I was picking up words) poured out the thick, sweet coffee and waddled out, shaking his bottom under his gown. "What remains are there of Ancient Egyptian religious beliefs in modern Egypt?"

"To be perfectly frank and candid with you, not much. Though there are certain links between the old religions and Christianity." Ashmuni was a Moslem. He was a gentle creature, with brown woolly hair and a brown woolly moustache; his hands were delicate, with long fingers. "Isis and Osiris, mother and child, virgin birth, death and resurrection. But that's all in the history of religion. The Ancient Egyptians had blue beads against the evil eye. So have we."

"But would a Copt want to revive any of the old religions?"

"No, it is impossible. They are Christians."

"Don't they climb pyramids and greet the sun, or anything like that?"

"Impossible. It would be against their religion."

"I've heard sacred prostitution took place in the temples and on the tops of pyramids."

"To be perfectly frank and candid with you, Mr. Cozens, religion isn't my field. You should read Dr. Budge on the subject. But I can tell you quite openly and without concealment it would have been impossible to do anything on top of a pyramid. It was covered with alabaster and, at least in Gizeh, came up to quite a sharp point."

"You mean sex didn't play a part in any of the Egyptian rites?"

"Not that I'm aware of. In Sumer and Babylonia, yes. But in the Nile Valley, no. Until the Persians and the Greeks came we were not a licentious people. Frankly, it was all very Victorian in old Egypt."

"There's no significance in a modern Egyptian climbing a pyramid?"

"Tourists climb pyramids. This is not a very interesting subject. Someone has been pulling your foot."

"Leg."

"Pulling your leg." He did not know how to take these questions. Just the sort of thing to interest a soldier. I could imagine him thinking; so I told him my uncle was married to a Coptic girl who had fallen off the Great Pyramid in the small hours of the morning. Ashmuni said he had never heard anything like it.

The whole thing was outrageous. Somebody had been lying to me.

No, I said, nobody had been lying, and Ashmuni remarked it was so odd that, if it really had happened, there must be some personal reason for it. There was nothing particularly Egyptian about throwing oneself off the Great Pyramid. In fact, it could be openly stated that suicide was a rarity in Egypt, like ghosts.

"Ghosts?"

"We have no ghosts. We are not haunted like the English. A Coptic woman married to an Englishman might be under severe family pressure. It would be worse than marrying – well, I was going to say a Jew or a Moslem, but that wouldn't be true. They have a great sense of racial purity, some of these families. I can imagine your uncle's marriage turning out unhappily for the lady. Quite honestly. If they stay in this country, that is."

"There's no family pressure."

"My young friend, how would you know? You have been teasing and joking with me all this time. You make fun. Very well. It is madness to be thinking all the time of the past when Egyptians should be thinking of the future. What is to become of us? Perhaps I upset you, but Germany will win this war. Hitler is very strong, sir. He says he will give us freedom. But will he? The English will go and the Germans will come. That is the only difference. I am being very blunt. What should I think about all this? What should I do?"

"I wasn't making fun."

"No?" He seemed a bit weary. "I sometimes believe you English despise us Egyptians so much you think there is nothing so bestial we won't do it. You have been mocking me. Speak frankly now, and candidly. Well, I believe you. When you see this lady say that Dr. Ashmuni of the Cairo Museum says her behaviour on the Cheops Pyramid has no religious significance."

"I can't do that. I'm not seeing her."

The next time I went to the Museum I said, "You mean you don't care who wins the war?"

Dr. Ashmuni shrugged. "Forgive me. You are upset."

If I was upset it wasn't for the reason he thought. I had been looking at the Goddess Nut again and thinking this was probably the only way I'd be able to see Nadia in the future. But Ashmuni supposed I must be thinking of the way the Afrika Corps was building up in the desert, German divisions were pushing into Russia, and that sort of thing.

"You wouldn't say the Germans had any kind of right on their side would you?"

"Right? Wrong?" Dr. Ashmuni could expel the cigarette smoke gently from between his thin lips and at the same time draw it up his nostrils. "States are powerful and therefore they fight. What has right or wrong to do with it?"

"What about the Jews?"

"Jews are a problem. When I was in Germany I saw Jews are a problem."

"These Nazis are criminals. This war is an anti-crime war. You can't say you're not against crime – and aggression and murder, and the rest."

Ashmuni smiled. "There is a lot of propaganda. Why do you find it so easy to believe it? I personally, frankly and candidly find it surprising you have not formed a more critical intelligence."

"You don't think there's much to choose between the Nazis and us?"

Ashmuni leaned forward so that his face was not a foot from mine. The cigarette smoke streamed out of his mouth and up his nostrils like an inverted waterfall. "Do you?" he said softly.

"Yes, I do. We're not so bad."

Nadia and the Goddess Nut interested me even more than the problem of evil at that moment; and this was the occasion when, after a number of questions, Dr. Ashmuni said that the Goddess's attitude was one of joy, welcome and protection. Dr. Ashmuni had, strange to realise, never seen the real Nadia. He certainly could not have known that when he explained Nut was welcoming the dead it was as much as to say that I, and not Uncle Raymond, was about to die.

So maybe Dr. Ashmuni was right and the Germans would

drive into Cairo. Nadia would be all right with her Egyptian passport. I would be dead all right; I wallowed in the thought.

"We're not so bad," I said to Dr. Ashmuni, and I imagined how Ronnie Penhaligon's face would have cracked into a smile to hear me say it. Unlike Penhaligon, though, I thought I had earned the right to make my little affirmation. So far as I knew, Penhaligon hadn't done dirt, he hadn't cuckolded an uncle, he hadn't let himself be used, he hadn't committed incest, he hadn't found himself as defenceless in love as a Medical Corps orderly had been defenceless in battle in the streets to Calais pier. He hadn't twisted as I had. So I finally stood up and said, "We are not so bad." Out of our many treacheries we make our little bit of loyalty.

Q.M.S. Razier said a chit had come in from G.H.Q. asking Colonel Patch whether I was officer material; the answer had to be no but what everyone was curious about was why G.H.Q. were interested. Razier explained that I was not officer material because I was in line for a couple of stripes and once I passed my Clerk, First Class, then I was in line for Warrant Officer and if the war lasted long enough and the casualties were as heavy as everyone expected there was no reason why, although I wasn't a doctor, I might not end up with a commission in the Medical Corps, as lieutenant-quartermaster which would mean I was in charge of all the stores in a General Hospital, than which – said Razier – there was no more cushy job. Anyway, that was roughly speaking why the Colonel didn't see his way to having that form filled in about my officer potential. The Colonel hadn't gone so far as to mention a lieutenant-quartermastership in the Medical Corps; what he had said was, "I'll have no bloody wire pulling in this H.Q."; but it left everyone with the feeling somebody had his eye on Private Cozens.

As for a straight transfer to a combatant unit, in the Middle East, that was not possible because I had not been through basic infantry training. Nobody was sending me back to the U.K. for that. They would if I got recommended to an O.T.C. but the Medical Corps view was that they wanted me where I was, and if I'd only shut up and tell my friend with a line on G.H.Q. that he had better lay off who knew, I might get not a couple but three stripes before the year was out.

I actually threw a registry file across the room and said I wasn't in for a commission, there had been some balls-up along the line, but if I couldn't get into a combatant unit I'd go sick with anxiety neurosis, as classified in the R.A.M.C. manual, "The Nomenclature of Diseases." The Armoured Corps would do, and I didn't need any training, I'd pick it up as I went along.

Whether it was Uncle Raymond who started this off, or Ibr. Guirgis at the races with General Auchinleck, this I never knew. Mr. Guirgis believed everything was possible between friends, even a King's Commission. The meeting in his box at Heliopolis Race Course with General Auchinleck did not take place. I knew it had been planned only when Mr. Guirgis, looking spry in white tennis shoes and a sporty looking check suit, said after the second race, "I am sorry but it looks as though the Commander-in-Chief is not coming. I wanted to bring you together." But of course Mr. Guirgis would have been quite capable of asking Auchinleck to give me a commission without a preliminary interview. He believed there was a special freemasonry between racegoers. So he may well have been behind this query from G.H.Q. He went into a lengthy explanation.

By this time I must have grown my moustache because I can remember Mr. Guirgis congratulating me on it, saying he was sure General Auchinleck would have welcomed this return to a fashion that gave so much character to the European face. He himself would have liked to grow a beard. Being a Copt he was not naturally hirsute. My moustache was large, coarse and springy like sandy-brown horsehair and was the most I could grow on my face without being put on a charge. It certainly made me look older. I would have liked to be really old, say twenty-five or six.

Mr. Guirgis's betting was minute, ten piastres a time, this being the minimum stake allowed and it was placed never on a horse but on the jockey; Rochetti was his favourite. He sent the coffee boy out with two ten piastre notes, one for himself, one for me, with instructions to place his money on Rochetti. And mine? Well, my money went on an elderly Australian jockey called Drummond who had, Mr. Guirgis told me with admiration, been warned off all the race courses of Europe. Neither of us ever won but as the horses came into the finishing straight, which was immediately below our box, Mr. Guirgis would stand up with the binoculars clapped to his eyes, moaning with excitement. Each race exhausted him. He would sit down, white-faced with shock and quite unable to speak.

After a couple of coffees he would lick his lips, wipe his glasses and say, "Rochetti is a Hungarian. He always wins at least one race." And out would come another ten piastre note from his wallet, like an addict's fee for another fix.

Betting, to him, was clearly not just a matter of winning or losing money on horses. If he had been a Calvinist I would have said the winning or losing of a bet was his sign. If Rochetti won, Mr. Guirgis could think of himself as one of the Elect, until the next race that is. And if Rochetti lost Mr. Guirgis was damned, once again until the next race. There was a cosmic drama on that scale going on in his mind, made all the more exquisite by the knowledge his personal merits did not influence the decision one way or the other. A win was grace. But Mr. Guirgis, who talked to me from time to time about theology, believed we got what we deserved in this life and the next one. God did not really speak to him through horse racing. But to witness Mr. Guirgis's agony as the horses came into the straight was to know how uncertainty could be cultivated for itself. It was his vice. It transported him. He did not know where he was or who he was. We lost a whole pound between us on the five races and Mr. Guirgis had been through five spiritual dramas.

"It is so unimportant," he said quietly, polishing his glasses and looking at me through worried old woman's eyes. "It is a day in the fresh air. Who would think there was a war on? Look at Lord Killearn talking to that jockey. The jockey doesn't come up to his top waistcoat button. And Lord Killearn is fat." Mr. Guirgis laughed. "It is like a man and a monkey. I am sure Lord Killearn thinks the jockey is a monkey." Mr. Guirgis was waving and trying to catch the British Ambassador's attention. He was free-wheeling back to normal.

"You'd get even more kick out of racing if you put on bigger bets."

"Oh no." He was quick and very serious. "The whole point is that it has to be unimportant."

"I don't see that."

"It is only because it is unimportant I can enjoy it. It is *just* bearable. If I made it important and put a lot of money on I should kill myself if I lost. Or somebody."

"You wouldn't kill yourself if you lost a lot of money."

"Yes, I might."

"Why do you attack people who go to Nadia's flat?"

Underneath this excitement about racing was a threat of violence; and now his talk had turned again to killing. He had talked casually of Uncle Raymond murdering Aunt Treasure. The words had not been empty.

"Is that what she says?"

"You attacked me and I had to hit back. I broke your teeth."

Mr. Guirgis looked quite stunned by this. He sat there in silence for quite a long time while I looked down at the throng of civilians and soldiers on that brilliantly sunny afternoon, quite a lot of women in long dresses and big hats, at Lord Killearn in the saddling enclosure bending down to hear what the jockey was saying; and men in smart suits and tarbooshes strolling up and down, clicking their strings of beads.

"I will not deny it," he said at last. "I did not, of course, know you were the soldier. I am naturally confused and upset. You did quite right to hit me. There are times when I should be hit."

"You must have thought I was somebody else."

"That's right," he said eagerly, "I thought you were somebody else."

In a mad sort of way, our agreeing he had intended to fell somebody else seemed to dispose of the question why he should want to fell anyone. He looked me squarely in the face-

80

laughing. "My dear young sir, so that was the first time we met!"

"I had no idea who you were. You just came at me out of the darkness."

He was laughing helplessly. "Oh dear, you did quite right to resist. What could I have been thinking of? But, as you say, I must have thought it was somebody else. It *must* have been somebody else I was thinking of. Because I didn't know you, Mr. Cozens. How could I possibly have intended to attack you? Clearly, there was nothing personal in it."

I laughed too. It was all a misunderstanding. No need to go into any greater detail. A certain amount of good had come out of the incident: fine new teeth for example.

"Honestly, Mr. Cozens, there are times when I am not myself. I think of your aunt's mother who is dead. I want to strike out against life. I am too old for a soldier or I would consider volunteering in some capacity, probably for the Free French. Now –" he looked at his race card – "for the next race I am going to abandon my friend Rochetti and go for Bogdaniche. I advise you to follow my example. He comes from somewhere in the Balkans. An excellent and very hard jockey. Ten piastres on Bogdaniche. Are you staying with Drummond?"

For all his gaiety and affected ease he had been really shaken and couldn't wait for the moment of ecstatic oblivion when the horses next came round the bend into the finishing straight.

From Port Tewfik, where he was now Embarkation Staff Officer, Uncle Raymond wrote saying that he had been reflecting on my behaviour. He could quite see I was a restless, ambitious youth who wanted to take a more active part in the war. So did he for that matter. It was his dearest wish to be posted to the Eighth Army. But there he was, at Port Tewfik, doing his bit and he hoped I would be equally patient. The language I had used to Aunt Nadia had horrified him. However, I wasn't to take that slap too seriously. Aunt Nadia, he had reason to believe, had been more amused than she seemed. When he was next able to get home he

81

would try and bring us together again, so that we could all be one happy family. But that was unlikely before the New Year. Meanwhile, this posing as an officer must stop.

I phoned Nadia to say I had received this letter. I had a week's leave coming up and thought of going to Upper Egypt, not to Luxor or Aswan, but to some quiet place where there was a chance I'd not see any uniforms. Could she suggest somewhere? I also said I'd been to the races with her father. The truth was I was just crazy to find some excuse to get in touch with her again.

"Yes," she said after a very long pause in which I judged she was reviewing my conduct at our last meeting. "I wouldn't be surprised if you could find somewhere like that."

I went round straight away and as soon as she opened the door I could see we were going to pretend that last meeting had not taken place; for she kissed me, immediately, on the lips and then stood back, holding my hands in hers, her arms extended.

"Put them straight up."

She looked surprised.

"Like that," I said, and showed her. She stood there, calm, wistfully smiling, her arms stretched above her head like the Goddess Nut in the museum welcoming the dead, so that her breasts were lifted under the cotton shift she was wearing.

"I like your moustache. It makes you look brave."

I soared on such a thermal of happiness I must have changed colour – perhaps I had turned white, like her father, when the horses came into the straight – because her eyebrows moved, just the tiniest bit, towards each other in concern, and she said, "I've been thinking about you."

"I was nervous about phoning. Your father didn't seem too put out. I mean he laughed it off."

"Laughed what off?"

"I told him I was the soldier who hit him."

She shrugged.

At the back of the flat was a small, rather dark room which

gave on to a street too narrow for motor traffic; it was cool and quiet in comparison with the south-west facing rooms over the heat and din of the Midan. We went and sat there in the most astonishing quietness. She opened a wooden box, inlaid with what looked like ivory and painted slats, and offered almonds encrusted with rough sugar crystals. I just didn't understand her. But she understood me all right and that seemed a more than adequate basis for the relationship. She really was a goddess and I a besotted worshipper.

"Your father says everybody is the same. National characteristics don't mean anything."

"He's wrong. People really are different." It was said neutrally but with tremendous authority. "It is arrogant to say people of different cultures are not different. And at the same time it's a bit pathetic, because it is just the sort of thing you'd expect a non-European to say when he's talking to a European. Europeans do not believe a Copt is like them. But a Copt says this because he wants to reassure himself that he is not inferior."

"You mean foreigners really are different?"

"Yes, and funny. Even absurd. That's how you and I seem to each other. Why pretend otherwise?"

"Your father says the best writers don't go in for funny foreigners."

"Don't trust writers, particularly the best ones. They fake the evidence to suit their own purposes, like Lawrence, or they are tailoring their fiction to the limitations of their readers." This must have come out of some essay she'd written when she was still Uncle Raymond's student. Once I thought they might even have been his ideas but I don't now. "That story by Henry James about a young man who had just published his first novel, and it was about some foreign country and the oddities of life there. Somebody said to him 'Next time, set your story in England, in a world we understand, so that we can measure it against our own experience.' That's a novelist's arrogance. You see what I mean? It shows up the limitations of fiction. You can't learn *anything* from it. It's an aesthetic experience, literature is. Anthropology and sociology, yes. That's where you get information from. Novels, no."

A girl who read anthropology and sociology, if that is what she was claiming, ought to have reacted to the discovery of the existence of Aunt Treasure with greater calm. But she hadn't read any of this stuff, she was just teasing; she didn't know a Trobriand Islander from a Hottentot, she was leading me on by implying nothing I'd read could prepare me for the experience of her. Her father was wrong. I wasn't to think of her as an English girl. She really *was* different, mysterious and a goddess. The talk was love play and it was really exciting.

She put a hand on my thigh and said, "We'll go to Upper Egypt together. I will tell my cousins you are my husband."

"But they'll know I'm not Uncle Raymond."

"They have never met him. You will wear your officer's clothes that Raymond told me about. You will be Professor Major Foulkes and I have it all worked out to the smallest detail because I have been thinking about it for some time. We go to Minia."

She made all things seem possible and I rose to this extraordinary proposition as though there was a real chance of our getting away with it.

"You ever been in England?" Even at moments of ecstasy I wanted to show I was still in control and could ask practical questions. In fact, I was – to use a much later expression – stoned out of my mind.

"No, we were going in 1937 but my mother died and there was the Munich crisis in 1938. So, no. I've been to Cyprus."

"Well, England is sort of –" I didn't know what it was sort of. I wasn't thinking about England. I was thinking of what she had said. Her husband! I soared like an eagle.

"I don't want to go to England. Ever."

"Why not?"

"I've a clear idea of England. I don't want it spoiled."

"From books. But you said you didn't believe in books."

"I accept", she said, "the authority of English writers when they are writing about England."

The combination of subjugation and reverence that makes up the relationship between the sexes is incomprehensible, more so than ever now that the memory of the physical pleasure has faded. How weird it all seems! I tore at her clothes. Literally. The cotton shift ripped like paper. Absolutely everything she wore, just tore and snapped like string and paper.

Other times we made love there was rage in it, her rage with Uncle Raymond and my rage with the army for not giving me a gun; unacknowledged rages at the time but, by God! I know now how deep below the surface those fires were burning, because I know how they were to break out. *But not then.* I didn't really know what was driving me. If I'd been asked I'd have said love. We were in a dream for most of the time. But on that occasion, the first time we had loved after she struck me, and the last before we went on that wild trip to the Coptic south, both of us crazy but in different ways, *then* – I swear, but there is no end to the self-deception one can get up to and I may be wrong – as we lay entwined there was no anger for anyone or anything else but only a melting and selfless tenderness for each other. I remember the brilliant, slavering happiness and the sense of unbounded freedom. This is how the gods felt.

"Anthropology," I said some time later, reverting to what her father had said about the exotic, "if you've got this scientific way of understanding things, I don't know why you should get so upstage about Uncle Raymond being married before."

"Can't you forget him for one moment?" This cut, and was meant to. "Cozens, darling –" in a whisper that seemed to exaggerate her high-class English vowels and plopping Ps and Bs – "Please be at the station by 9 o'clock. Myself I will buy the first-class tickets. It is something to take my husband to the heart land of my people." Odd to reflect she never called me anything but my surname.

"I get a warrant to go on leave."

"I myself will get the tickets." She was standing, quite naked, in front of a wall mirror staring at herself with no expression on her face at all that I could detect, gently massaging her ribs below her breasts as though I had bruised her there: but calm. and in a mad sort of way welcoming in the way the Goddess Nut was welcoming. She was studying herself, so it could scarcely have been me she was welcoming.

Razier had been quite unexpectedly commissioned and told to stand by for a posting. He did not expect still to be in Cairo when I came back from leave, so he said, "Tell you what, we'll go out on the town. I'll have my pips up but you needn't let that worry you, not just for one night. We won't do anything ostentatious." With his disability he did not expect a posting into the desert, which is what he would have liked. He had a notion he was being sent to some cushy job in South Africa, at the transit base. He said South Africa was a sexually respectable country and before he left Egypt he wanted to patronise a certain Officers' Only whore who apparently did it all in some style. "She's what you'd call a courtesan, really," he said. "You know, she goes in for conversation. I won't actually do anything, you know. It's the personality of that sort of woman that interests me. And the conversation. Cozens boy, it's smashing to be an officer."

We took a tram to an open-air restaurant where we drank beer in the light of pink electric lanterns hung on ropes between the palm trees. Beyond Gizeh a red glow in the sky was extinguished and that was sunset. The night was dark blue. The smell of dank, irrigated earth hung in the air. You could sense grapes, the prickly pear and maize growing in the dark. Fields and gardens came right into the city where we were. The feluccas on the Nile had oil lamps on their masts; we were near enough to the river to feel the coolness of the water on our faces and see these nocturnal lamps moving between the black palms.

"You don't want to take too much initiative in the army, see," said Razier. He came from Bromley and spoke a special kind of flat cockney which made him sound as though he was always complaining. This was far from being the case. "I'm a regular and

I know what I'm saying. Don't push your luck. You're just a kid. You and me probably won't meet after tonight. Well, that's all right. I'm an officer. Maybe we'll meet. Maybe we won't. But my advice to you is don't push your luck."

"Luck?"

"You came out of Calais and I came out of Calais, but that's bloody well not good enough for you. You want to get in a combatant corps. If you go on pressing your luck and trying to get into a combatant unit you'll end up dead, and you're a bloody long time dead, son. Forget it."

"You think when you're dead you're dead?"

"That's absolutely right. Shall I tell you something? I never knew my old man, my dad, because he was killed on the Somme not long after I was born. And I tell you something, when you're a nipper and you grow up with your father being dead, do you know what you do? You hate him. I always hated my dad because he was dead. I felt he'd sort of let me down because other kids had dads but he'd got killed. He just wasn't there and I hated him for it. It's true. You ever hate anybody? I mean really hate them, like I hated my dad?"

"Yes, I hate my Uncle Raymond."

Razier said, "It was silly me hating my dad because he wasn't there for me to hate, but I reckon we've all got to hate somebody or we'd finish up hating ourselves."

"I don't know why you hated your dad."

"He'd sort of slid out and left my ma and me to cope on our own. He was all right because he knew nowt about it."

"It wasn't his fault."

"What's that got to do with it? He wasn't there, that's all. I didn't believe in God or I might have hated Him. Why d'you hate your uncle, then?"

"He's just a shit, that's all."

"They could send me to bloody India," Razier said after a long pause. "And because of my hip I won't see any field service so there are none of the allowances. My old girl'll be tickled pink, me an officer; but there's not all that much money in it. I did three years in India."

"My Uncle Raymond's a real bastard."

"You've got to hate somebody, otherwise it's all turned in on yourself. I've seen chaps in the army get religious mania because they couldn't hate anybody. Do you know what happens if you can't hate anybody? You feel guilty. It rots you. My ma was upset because dad's name was blacked out on the war memorial. That was me did it. I never told her."

"That's twisted."

"No, that's not twisted, that's healthy, and if you can talk like that, son, you've no idea. You don't know what I'm on about, see? Your dad's alive and kicking, I've no doubt."

"Yes."

"Well, you're lucky it's only your uncle you've got it in for."

"Yeah, I hate him, I reckon." I said, "and I feel sorry for him, really."

"Son, this war is too big to buck. It's fate. Keep your head down."

"Thanks."

"Strictly speaking, war is for sods like me not the likes of you. Now, you ought to be in college."

"What's different between you and me?"

"I'm a regular. Now, about this courtesan, see? Time's short. But you can't just go along to this bird, you've got to make an appointment and if she don't like the sound of your voice you don't get one."

"Where does she live, then?"

He produced his diary. There was not enough light from the lantern so he struck a match and the air was so still the flame did not flicker. "Mrs. Foulkes," he said, after a while, pronouncing the word Fowlks. "What a puking name! 5, Midan Ismailia. Telephone number 67342."

"That's my auntie. It's pronounced Folks."

"Then you've the top courtesan in Cairo in the family. She's a red lady. Not your ordinary bint at all. But you don't say! No wonder you don't like your uncle. Mind you, it's nothing to be ashamed of. *Don't take it so bad now.* Get a grip of yourself. Hey! It puts me off though, knowing she's your auntie."

chapter 5

Mr. Guirgis took up golf out of admiration for P.G. Wodehouse; the stories Wodehouse's Mr. Mulliner told in the club house created, he said, a most nice and agreeable world. Mr. Guirgis too, at times, wanted to enter this nice world. Because of the racing he was already a member of the Gezireh Sporting Club; so once the decision to play golf had been taken he had, in 1938, bought a bag of clubs and placed himself in the hands of the professional there, a Scot called Jonson who had now gone home; Mr. Guirgis was currently playing to a handicap of 14. He had me out on the Sporting Club course with a borrowed bag of clubs and two Sudanese caddies.

Mr. Guirgis said I had a natural style and he told Mr. Mulliner-type stories about other men with a natural style; one had come to a bad end because he hadn't been reverential enough about his gifts and it all led to his not marrying some pasha's daughter and even being kicked out of the Turf Club. Then there was another chap who – but what it all amounted to was that golf brought happiness not to the naturally endowed but to the mediocre, like Mr. Guirgis himself, who worked hard to improve themselves. What particularly irked him was that I hit the ball so well when I held the club in the wrong way. I was right-handed but my left hand grasped the club below my right hand.

He wore leather straps on his thin wrists to give them greater strength, a Fair Isle pullover and white cotton breeches cut like jodhpurs; he wore, too, a white cap with a big peak, very large blue-tinted glasses and, as usual on all his sporting occasions, the white tennis shoes. He seemed old, frail and spindly in the manner of some great abandoned insect, a laggard locust or a spent cicada, waiting for the flutter and smother of great wings and the flashing beak.

"Horse racing is different," he said. "There you know you have to do with matters affecting human destiny – I mean vigour and strength and chance and breeding and corruption, not to speak of actual crime. To be obsessed with horse racing is to be obsessed with something that tells you about life itself. I see it is an analogue. Betting is my way into that analogue. My entrance ticket is bought cheaply. I do not gamble heavily. It is enough for my purpose. But golf is another matter. Clearly it is not an analogue. From the point of view of a sensible man it is not important; but it provides opportunities for persuading him that it is. Every sensible man must have some triviality that he can take seriously.

"Provided", said Mr. Guirgis in his Mr. Mulliner manner as he rejected the club offered by his caddy and peered short-sightedly at the alternatives, "that if this triviality is a game like golf he does not lose sight of the larger game of being absolutely serious in the knowledge that, in the last resort, golf is not serious at all."

"It's exercise." I couldn't make anything of his paradoxical way of talking.

"Exercise!" Mr. Guirgis looked at me. I could see that Mr. Guirgis was wondering what Mr. Mulliner would have gone on to say. "A man who plays golf for exercise isn't taking it seriously enough."

This was not bad. What Mr. Guirgis actually said must have been something like, "Fitness and good health, oh dear no, sir, they are not right targets. They are wrong targets. Good golfers don't mind about exercise. They fix their minds on more trivial matters."

"Golf," said Mr. Guirgis, so memorably that the words have stuck, capital letters and all, "is not a Life Analogue. It's more of an Evasion."

There were a lot of players on the course, most of them business men of European stock in white shorts or export-only plus fours; but there was a sprinkling of the military, in khaki or blue drill, as busy with their horsetail fly-whisks as they were with their clubs. At that time the Egyptians themselves hadn't seemed to go in for golf. They were more for squash and swimming. Anyway, because of the crowd we had to wait in the flies and the thick afternoon sunlight, talking of playing games. Was the war itself the biggest game of all?

Abruptly I told him I was going on leave to Upper Egypt and Nadia was going with me. We were going to marry as soon as it could be arranged, Uncle Raymond or no Uncle Raymond. Deal with that, Mr. Mulliner! Mr. Guirgis stood with his legs apart studying me through his blue-tinted lenses, apparently shrunken with shock. It was like hitting him for a second time. And, in my innocence, I had wanted his help. Give some reassurance! Say Nadia is a good, sweet, shy and much abused young lady! Dispel my nightmare! Please, Mr. Mulliner, some comfort!

I didn't get any. Recovering from his numbness, Mr. Guirgis jumped like a frog and brought his heels together, wagged his club and said it was all a great joke. He giggled through his clenched teeth and swung fiercely at the tee-ed up ball in an uncalculating way that caused it to fly off at an angle and lodge in the knobbly trunk of a palm tree. One of the caddies had to climb up and get it.

"Hee! Hee! Hee!" Mr. Guirgis began theorising in what he probably thought was Mr. Mulliner's style, about the Egyptian character and its sense of fun and fantasy. "It is impossible for us to improve our condition by anything we do. We are prisoners of history. So we have fantasies. But nothing happens. We don't find any buried treasure. We don't win at the races. We make gestures but they do not mean anything. You talk of going to Upper Egypt with Nadia and marrying her. You won't. Nothing will happen. The country will not let you. You will still be talking about it in a month's time. You will talk of it in a year's time. No one is deceived, except possibly you. Nadia is not deceived. Nothing will happen. She knows it, and I know it, we all know it, but you don't know it because you are –"

He hesitated, and then giggled and shrugged his shoulders.

"Still English." I said. "You were telling me there was no difference between the English and Egyptians."

"No, I said, only that you had to think and act *as though* there was no difference. Like Shakespeare. We are jolly people, in fact, Mr. Cozens. What you have told me about going to Upper Egypt reminds me of that story in *The Thousand Nights and One Night*. This beggar of Baghdad is deceived by a rich and beautiful girl into thinking he is to have intercourse with her. He is bathed and fed. The servants show him what they say is the door to the lady's bedroom. Quite naked, and with a big erection, the beggar rushes through this door in a great excitement, only to find himself in the street with crowds of people laughing at him. The beautiful girl, and her friends and servants, are looking down on him from a window and laughing too. But who is to say that just before he rushed through that door the beggar had not in anticipation as much joy as he would in the fulfilment of his lust? And you, Mr. Cozens, in your anticipation, you are as happy now as you will ever be. Isn't that a serious thought? You will never be happier than you are at this minute. And it is all based on an expectation of something that will never happen."

"It's not like that."

"How are you going to Upper Egypt? You are going to meet at the station? It will be like in the story. Nadia will not be there. Or, really, she will not be on the platform. She will be up in the station master's window, laughing. The station master is Marouf Bey, a good friend of ours, and this is just the sort of prank he would enjoy. Nothing will happen."

"It's not like that at all." Now that he couldn't reassure me I was going to tell *him*. "Officers go to her flat. She's not like you think. Being shocked because she was Uncle Raymond's concubine is rubbish. It doesn't make any difference to me. Do you understand that? *Can you?* I just want her. Everything will be different and she'll be changed, and I'll be changed." I must have squeaked with round-eyed hysteria.

He was laughing at me now, Mr. Guirgis was, tee-heeing, and sniggering and giggling and wiping his nose with the back of his

92

hand and taking off his blue-tinted glasses as though to get a closer look at me out of those small, bloodshot, tear-blurred eyes. "Who tells you officers go to her flat?"

"Why else were you waiting on the stairs? You thought I was one of those officers. I expect she's on some Officers' Only directory. Everybody knows. I don't care. It doesn't matter to me. It's all going to be different. Nobody understands Nadia, but I understand her. No, that's not right. I don't care if I don't understand her."

"Haven't you any jealousy?"

"I'm not the jealous type, I reckon."

"At the nineteenth hole," said Mr. Guirgis in his P.G. Wodehouse manner, "we'll have a couple of coffees and talk this over because I can see you're in danger of *a scrape*." It was as though, in his imagination, I had some rich aunt who would cut me out of her will if I married Nadia and that was the extent of the problem. He had to use his handkerchief to wipe the tears of laughter from his eyes.

This was how I found I could hate Mr. Guirgis too; I dropped my club and walked off.

On my way back to barracks Major Penhaligon hailed me across the tramlines. He came over and said, "You've been much on my mind since our last meeting. I think we should go off and pray together in the Cathedral –" we were outside the Anglican cathedral – "but I'm on my way to be photographed. Why don't you come along and watch? He's a very interesting man."

"No, thanks, I've got to get back."

"It's on the way." He talked me into walking to Kasr el-Nil but I didn't need a lot of persuading because, after all, he was an old friend of Uncle Raymond's and might have some angle on Nadia. There was not much time. I didn't believe Mr. Guirgis's claim that she would not turn up the following morning. He talked of fantasy and self-deception but he was the last person to do that, really; or perhaps he was just proving his own generalisation. There was no limit to what Egyptians would believe if it made them comfortable.

"What man?"

"He's a Hungarian, very intellectual. Jewish, I suppose. This photo is to send back to my wife in the States."

We went up in a lift and the photographer turned out to be a plump middle-aged man with eyes that seemed swollen from crying, who said he had just been photographing Major Randolph Churchill and he was just a big baby. He gave us tea. While we drank it Major Penhaligon said he was a believer in the now unfashionable view that character showed itself in the face.

"Cozens, here, is going through a crisis. He believes he is responsible for the universe. Can't you see the torture in his face? And, of course, the arrogance."

"No," said the photographer, whose name turned out to be Léon, "I don't see any torture or arrogance. He's a pretty boy." He patted me on the cheek making a moue with his lips. Those swollen eyes were deceptive. He was quite jolly. "I think it's very nice to see a young man with a conscience."

"Léon," said Penhaligon, "will you do me a favour? Take Cozens's photograph now and then take it again after we've had a prayer together."

"I'm not having any praying in here."

"But he's a damned soul. He's in hell. Look at him. Look at the blackness and despair."

Léon actually came over and kissed me on the cheek. "He's absolutely sweet and I'm not having any praying here, I tell you, because I don't really believe in it."

"I wanted a picture of him before prayer and another photo of him after. Before and after treatment. It's all in the interest of religion. Now, you're Jewish, aren't you? You must be in favour of religion."

"I'm not having any praying in this apartment."

"Hell's teeth, man! Then, just take his photograph. I'll pay."

"Before I take yours?"

"Sure, before you take mine. I tell you this is an interesting scientific experiment."

Léon took me into his studio and made me pose with my chin in the air. He studied me through his view-finder, shook his head

94

sadly, and said, "Your neck looks wrong. Put this round your throat."

He produced a gaily coloured kerchief and tied it round my throat, presumably with the intention of making me look less gangling. Then he switched on all the lights and I could see him and Major Penhaligon only as indistinct shapes on the other side of the brilliance. But I could hear Penhaligon saying, "Isn't that exactly what you'd imagine Judas Iscariot looked like?"

When Léon had taken a half a dozen or so exposures, Penhaligon said, "Have you done, now? Cozens, come with me."

And although Léon screamed angrily after us he led me out of the front door, closing it behind us, and flopped on his knees on the landing in front of the iron grille that enclosed the lift shaft.

"Pray with me, Dave," he said, in solemn voice. "On your knees, son."

I did this. In spite of Penhaligon I thought, yes, it would be good to pray because there was just no one to turn to; it was more important to get supernatural reassurance than to resist Penhaligon's crackpot idea of procuring before and after photographs to demonstrate just how good he was in the prayer business.

"Dear God," said Penhaligon, "look down in compassion on Dave, this troubled young man. Reveal to him that life is not so complicated as he imagines. Show him there are forces of darkness and there are forces of light. It is for him to choose."

"This is all rubbish," I said. "I don't believe in God."

"Help his unbelief," Penhaligon intoned, his hands together and pointing the prayer to the ceiling, his eyes closed. The lift rose up the shaft and, as it passed, I was aware that an old man with a heavy, square, pale face like a worn paving stone was studying us sadly as he went sailing up to a higher floor. He seemed so unsurprised to see two men on their knees that he must have been used to the sight. As used to it as God was, I thought. Perhaps he was God.

Léon opened the door of his flat. "Just as I thought," he said.

"Praying! I won't have it. I'm not taking any more photographs of that young man."

Penhaligon was furious. "Dammit man, we haven't darned well finished our act of devotion. Now, leave us alone! We have business with our Father."

"Not outside my apartment, you haven't. I'll speak to Major Churchill. Stop it at once, now."

But Penhaligon would not stop. He went on praying for my salvation, the lift whirred and clicked in its shaft, Léon began to scream again and the porter, way down below, called up from his ground-floor cubby-hole, asking what was going on. It was difficult to know why Léon was so much against praying.

Penhaligon opened his eyes and pointed at me. "Look, the winter is passing, the ice is melting, the water is beginning to flow, the log jam breaks, and love and happiness begin to move on the face of this young man. Léon," he cried, "you owe it to mankind to photograph Cozens as he now looks and document the healing powers of prayer."

"I can't photograph anybody on the landing, Major Penhaligon, and in any case I do not know what is going on."

"Dave! Back into the studio! You're transformed, lad."

"God's upstairs," I said.

"What?"

"He went up in the lift. I saw him."

Penhaligon was thoughtful, rather as though he was wondering whether his praying had been a bit too powerful, and he had overdone the whole thing.

"God isn't anywhere physically, Dave," he said gently.

"I saw him go up in the lift. He had a square white face."

"No, no. Let us go into Léon's flat and have one of his cups of tea. We must talk about this. What a pity your Uncle Raymond is not here to see you."

"I hate him," I said, "and I hate you."

"It is a sign of the damned that they hate the light, and they hate virtue. Your Uncle has been much put upon. One day you'll understand. As for you and your present state, no one will be able to help you until you have sounded the depths of your own despair." He breathed out noisily through his large, horse-like nose. "When that happens, write to me c/o the Chaplain-General's department and we shall take up our praying where we left off. The experiment," he said to Léon, "has been a failure. You can see with your own eyes that I have been deceived. No change has come about. All is black and despairing as it was before. The Devil has him by the throat, and you sensed it by trying to hide the wound with that cloth. You cannot hide the Devil's marks. Léon, it is no good trying to photograph him again now. It would be a waste of time." He shouted after me, "I love you. It is a mark of maturity to love even when the love is not returned; when hate is returned even."

"Don't flatter yourself!" I yelled as I hurtled down the stairs, not waiting for the lift in case God was still in it.

Fighting Razier would have put me in the glass house and meant not meeting Nadia at Cairo station the following morning. Him with his broken hip, I'd nail him one day, the obscene liar. But was he? On a hot evening I trembled with cold. I had no wisdom. I knew nothing.

There were thoughts of Uncle Raymond's sister, my mother. The week's washing bubbled in the copper, the house reeked of soda and steam. Her arms were red to the elbow. What could she know of a sister-in-law, or a daughter-in-law, what kith was she with a girl who talked of Henry James and fornicated on an Officers Only basis, myself excepted? What could *I* know, for that matter? Nothing!

"No joking." Razier looked worried. "I had no idea she was your auntie. It's a striking coincidence, and not for the first time. A chap was posted to my regiment in India and we got talking. He was born in the same house that I was. We didn't know each other. Not the same age, mind you. Years between us. If you could only understand what lay behind coincidence I reckon you'd know something really important. How was I to know Mrs. Foulkes was your auntie? Your name isn't Foulkes."

His horrible story was plausible because it was implausible. Courtesan, he said. The word hit hard. If, for a young man, there is a choice between anger befitting ignorance and the credulity appropriate for a man of the world he chooses credulity every time. He's a sucker for anything that reveals human nature to be coarser than anything he'd come across. Yes, he believed his mistress was a whore! So what! With real tears running down his face he said, so what? He didn't want to be thought a rustic innocent.

"You've got to allow for foreign behaviour," said Razier when I argued there'd been some mistake. Nadia was so monogamic she had given my uncle a rough time because he'd been married before. "Neither you nor me understand foreign behaviour, see? 'Course a foreign bint wouldn't want to be a concubine, then finding out she was and going the whole hog."

"She's not a concubine."

"She thinks she is and if she thinks she is it comes to the same thing. If I'm your concubine, she says to your uncle, I'm the Cairo town whore too and what does that make you? In Quetta I knew a squaddie set up a whore in a room, paid the rent and that, to be his own respectable bird with no other blokes involved. You know what? She cut his throat because he'd made her respectable. She did him in! She really did! It's the opposite of your auntie. She's on the game to humiliate your uncle, see? Tell you something else. Your uncle knows all about this little caper."

"He doesn't know a blind thing."

"How could your auntie humiliate him if he didn't know anything about it? In Hong Kong the Ser'nt-Major's bird wrote anonymous letters saying what a bitch she was, so that when he taxed her she got on her high horse and said he had a dirty mind. All done to wound. That's what life's made up of mostly, particularly from women, because they don't like being taken for granted." After a pause for thought Razier said, "One thing, mate, it takes your mind off the war."

The young in general don't like being taken for granted. One of their great motives is to be thought incomprehensible and disgusting. Only a hick failed to disgust. Nothing should be allowed to stand in the way of freedom, maturity and disillusionment. Nothing, to be blunt about straightforward lust and ecstasy, should be allowed to stand in the way of pleasure. Yet even more important than gratification was the need for cynicism. Growing that filthy moustache was an expression of the need. A bit more simplicity all round, a readiness to confess plain and contempt-ible innocence, and things might have turned out better. But we are always offering each other up, as Nadia was offered up, on the altar of striving after worldly wisdom. Today, I am clean-shaven.

Only a father could understand outraged chastity – if that is what it was – on the scale Nadia played it and still pretend he didn't. Not a husband. Not a lover. Neither of them could do it. If Mrs. Guirgis had still been alive Mr. Guirgis might have been less devious. Maybe not. Fathers of daughters have, at the best of times, I guess, an ambiguous role; a puzzling mixture of doing and not doing, of knowing and not knowing. King Lear did really know all the time that Cordelia loved him; he couldn't admit it because he was a father and there's a rule for fathers – never let on you know as much as your daughter.

Mr. Guirgis waiting on the stairs knew why he was waiting; Mr. Guirgis on the golf course at the Sporting Club couldn't do anything but act as though he didn't know. Here was a muddle tragedy could spring from. A husband seems less likely to have conflicting and irreconcilable pictures of the woman than a father does, and it was Uncle Raymond's fate to be more of a father than a husband. To Nadia he was a bit of a Daddy. Perhaps he felt paternal and compounded the muddle. But why should he worry? His sufferings made him a kind of saint and, deep down, that is all he wanted from life. It is not my idea of sainthood. Saints have to be more than long-suffering; they have to choose their role, not let it be forced on them. Lovers choose. Appearances are against it, but I still believe they choose. Any-way, they choose after their fashion. So far as I'm concerned fatherhood is a matter of speculation, but about lovers I know.

In spite of circumstances I swear that, at that time, Nadia and I enjoyed all the usual twangling of a transfiguration. I won't be cheated out of believing we were changed.

The train left about nine and I didn't arrive at the station until it was just about to go because there was a difficulty over the travel voucher, and I was held up. I'd forgotten Nadia had said she would get the tickets. The Company office would not give me a voucher for Minia because, they said, it was out of bounds to troops. It wasn't a bit of good claiming I had an invitation to stay with friends; the sergeant said he wasn't providing any leave chits for Minia, not to O.C. Troops himself and I ought to have known better than to ask. He wrote me out a voucher, stamped it and said, "This'll take you to Luxor. If you get out on the way that's your affair." Then I couldn't find a taxi.

Nadia in a fury was standing opposite the first-class coach. Her face seemed smaller and whiter than usual, her nostrils were pinched, her mouth really quite tiny and set. She hissed at me, "Why are you late? I have a seat but there is no room for you. You will have to stand in the corridor. Look!"

It was true there was no room. She had to push her way back on to the train, past peasant women in black with huge baskets and babies, men eating bread and boiled eggs, climbing over corded boxes and cases and cages with young chicks in them, to the corner seat that a black-hatted, bearded orthodox Jew was preserving for her by arching his body over it, his forearms flat against the back of the compartment to take the strain of any pressure the mob fighting to get in through the far window might put on him.

The journey south! I had imagined Nadia and me sitting side by side. The flat countryside, the palm groves, the canals and beyond them the sandy hills and cliffs, all these would slide by in a light so intense they seemed the thinnest water colour; so thin the texture of the paper showed through as some profounder reality – I supposed – would appear in our own relationship once I could say "Nadia, you don't have to explain anything. I know everything but I love you. You love me. This is our honeymoon. That is all that matters." I imagined myself talking like that for the hour or so it would take to get to Minia, but we couldn't talk at all.

The journey took not an hour or so but a good five. It would be an exaggeration to say I hadn't enough room to stand. I had. The soles of my shoes made contact with the floor, but I had to bend my body sideways at the hips to accommodate, on the one side a veiled woman with a huge unmanœuvrable elbow stuck out and on the other a legless man on a little wheeled trolley whose head, for most of the journey, rested against my thigh. The windows were open.

After a hundred miles or so a sandstorm blew up and the air turned amber. It soon seemed I had been there in that reeking corridor since the beginning of time and it was my fate to remain there for ever. The girl I loved was near but unattainable. In any case she hated me and was a calculating, lascivious beast (I had already lost my bogus worldliness) and she was the most monstrous hypocrite there had ever been. She was sick. She was evil. And I was sick and evil too. No one would have pity on us. We were together for ever in this parching sandstorm, but unable to communicate. Even in the choking, goat-like stink of the storm there was a powerful reek of human beings: sweat, breath, urine, faeces. The cheep! cheep! of chicks and the wailing of babies were unceasing. The journey was for ever! This was Hell!

We stopped at some remote station and the wind hissed about us like snakes. On the platform a man loomed out of the golden murk and if it had been the Devil himself, with cloven hoof and tail and the shining beauty of the damned, it would not have been surprising. But it was only Mr. Guirgis! It really was. I knew him by his sucked-in cheeks and specs. He was changed, though. He seemed enormous in the storm. It was as though the shifting, hot air was a lens and through its magnification he appeared not as the insect-like victim I had thought him to be at the Sporting Club but as himself a predator, so huge that the train, the scurrying figures on the platform and the palms whipping against the sky were absurdly out of scale.

"Impossible." At Minia station Nadia looked about. "My father never comes to Minia. There is an old quarrel."

Certainly, there was no sign of him. We were through the sandstorm and the air was pearly and quiet. With such a crowd, though, it would have been easy for him to disappear into the station buildings. When I told Nadia I was pretty sure her father was on the train she stood there on the platform, women with baskets and shouting men, all milling around her, the sun, strong even through the haze, above and behind so that her face was shaded by the wide brim of her hat and her eyes all the larger for it, just looking at me, intent, wary, motionless. The baked air was still gritty. She was wearing a very loose white cotton over-garment, a travelling coat to protect her clothes from the kind of filth she saw herself surrounded by on journeys – she was always fastidious – and this loose cloak had a hood which she now lifted over her head, hat and all. She might have been wearing a bridal crown. Indeed, all in white, with the sun beating down from behind her head she was bride-like and expectant and very still in a way I knew would prove unforgettable. The very vagueness of the strong impression is why it comes back so vividly. What were we doing there? Who were we? I can remember that doubt and that alarm.

"There is still time for you to get back on the train and go to Luxor, if that is what you want, so as not to waste the full value of your ticket. Goodbye!" And she would have walked off with the porter who was clutching both our bags.

"No, but we can't say I'm my uncle." I had the appropriate crowns up on my shoulder. It wasn't the military side of the deception that now seemed difficult to carry off. Nadia had a couple of civvy shirts, a jacket and some trousers she had bought especially for the occasion. Together with her own things they were now in that big brown case. I could walk about pretending I was a civvy; and I was confident enough, now that I had grown a moustache, of being accepted as a university teacher. The thing could be done. But it seemed audacious and unnecessary, particularly as Mr. Guirgis was probably in the offing.

A big woman in black, screaming like an express train, bore down on Nadia and clutched her in her arms. Behind her was a little, unshaven man in a yellowing cotton suit and a tarboosh, who was thoughtfully smoking a cigarette in a long holder. When his eyes caught mine he smiled, but he immediately turned his gaze elsewhere, flicked the ash off his cigarette and sighed deeply. These were Nadia's cousins, Mari and her husband, Yusif the dentist – trained, he was soon to tell me, at Grenoble and it was to France he would wish to return when the war was over.

"Mari says my father is definitely not here." Nadia and her cousin had been talking in Arabic for some time. "Mari says that if he were within five miles of her she would know it by the way her skin itched."

Mari had a colourless, rather puffy face. It flushed far back, under the ears when she was excited, leaving the front more like a mask than ever. "He did not invite me to your wedding, even." She put her head back and shouted these words, snatched at my shoulders and kissed me to the right and left of my mouth, moistly and smelling of pistachio nuts. There was something a bit forced about the greeting, as if she knew I was bogus, but didn't want to admit it even to herself.

"Welcome to El Minia," said Yusif, shaking me by the hand and smiling into my face before transferring his gaze to some point over my head as he exhaled an incredible amount of smoke. "Not much of a place, I'm afraid. It is not like a European city. All the detail is slipshod – the door handles, the keyholes, the window frames."

"You look very young," said Mari, staring at me.

"We thought we'd have a drive around first," said Nadia, "before coming to the house. We had a really nasty, crowded journey."

"He is certainly a very young professor," said Yusif to no one in particular and although nobody laughed there was the feeling of a joke being savoured. "We Egyptians have no sense of structure, only mass. By mass," he said, "I mean – well, something big, you see, like a pyramid. But the Eiffel Tower has structure. It grieves me that the Eiffel Tower is now in the hands of the Germans. I am not like many other Egyptians, Professor Foulkes – or should I call you Major Foulkes? – who want the Germans to win this war so that we can throw off the imperialist yoke as we would have been free if only Napoleon had stayed in our country and freed us from the tyrannical Mamelukes. Not at all. I admire Mr. Churchill. I think the Eiffel Tower is the most beautiful structure in the world and I am sorry to say that no Egyptian could have built it because we Egyptians have no sense of structure." And so on. Once the ice had been broken he chattered away as we moved down the platform behind Nadia and her cousin.

"Don't talk politics with Yusif," said Nadia when we were seated in a gharry, swaying and creaking through the shuttered town. "He will get himself into trouble." Yusif and Mari had taken our bags home in a taxi while Nadia carried out her plan to take the air; in reality it was to have a row.

"It is too late to change. They wouldn't understand. They would be bewildered."

"I can't pretend to be Uncle Raymond, that's all."

"You don't love me," she screamed. "You hate me! You despise me! You've been spying on me."

I tried to draw her closer. Her thigh pressed against mine and there was so much sexual excitement and anger being generated we just didn't care where we were, in this horse-drawn gharry rocking along at not much more than a walking pace, so that curious spectators could actually keep up and watch us clawing and pushing at each other. Nadia shouted something in Arabic to the driver who began laying about him with his whip. The gharry picked up speed and the crowd's curiosity turned to jeering and abuse. The sight of an Egyptian woman with a soldier excited them no end. There was simply bound to be trouble.

"It's just because I love you I don't want to pretend to be Uncle Raymond."

"You *must* be." She spat the words out. "You are here as my husband, we are man and wife. Do you think I'm a loose woman to sleep here, in El Minia, with a man who is not my husband?"

"You mean it's different in Cairo?"

"But of course."

The town was a distance from the river. The crowd was left behind. We drove, through a cloud of dust, down an avenue of eucalyptus trees with flaked trunks and turned, slowly and uncertainly, along a dirt track on the very bank of the river which was vast and clear like a lake. The far bank seemed miles away. Over there were miniature palms and a miniature mud village with a whitewashed dome catching the sun and pointing at us a faint reflection over the water. The sweet smell of the river was detectable even through the gharry's peculiar reek of horse manure and crushed bugs. A hot, sweet, enormous, open world of water, air, rushes, cane and vast green fields rocked past.

"Let's go to Luxor."

"Why are you such a coward? I want you here. You are my husband. Even if I am killed I want it here, with you as my husband. I've been a whore. That's what you've found out."

"Could be. What do you mean, killed? Who would kill you?"

"Could be, you say! Why am I so hungry? Perhaps I'm pregnant."

"That's not funny."

"Do you think I'm joking? Understand this, Cozens. You might not be the father. Or Raymond. That disgusts and shocks you, but that's because you're a man and you don't understand how the only weapon a woman's got to use in this society is her sex. Samson had his strength to pull down the temple, but I've only got my sex and the power of procreation and the willingness to die –" She ran out of breath and made a funny howling noise in her throat.

"I don't care if you've been a tart," I said. "It means nothing to me."

"Then it should do."

"You're not pregnant, either. Don't try to give me that. You're not daft."

"You tell me what I am and what I am not." She climbed down from the gharry and I had the idea she might be preparing to throw herself into the Nile. "That's very cheeky."

"Don't talk in such a silly, exaggerated way then."

She screamed. "You called me a tart!"

"I don't care what you've done, that's what I'm saying. O.K., I understand you. It wasn't because you enjoyed it. It certainly wasn't for the money. You just wanted to do dirt on Uncle Raymond. That's all right with me too. It's all in the past. Forget it!"

"You're a pig."

I jumped down after her but she snatched the whip out of the driver's hand and gave the nag a flick across the buttocks. It moved off with a jerk but the driver brought it under control before it had moved more than a few yards. He was an old stick of a man with a week's silvery growth on his sunken cheeks. Nadia refused to let him have the whip back, even after he had scrambled down from his high seat and scampered back along the track towards her, not angry as I had expected, but making cajoling sounds, stretching out his hands and clicking his fingers. Nadia would have none of it. She laughed, lifted the whip and made, clumsily, to slash me across the face but I closed with her and held her hard, my arm round her waist.

"If we go to my cousins now and say you are not my husband after all, what will they say?" She wasn't angry at all, really. I saw it was impossible to make her angry.

"We've got a problem. I can see that. But don't let's lose sight of the fact we came here to sleep together."

I took the whip from her and threw it in the direction of the driver. As always happened when our bodies were close, or touching, as they were now, the happiness just exploded inside us. I made her take off that big brimmed hat and we stood repeatedly kissing each other on the face, on the lips, idiotically laughing. I must have said something about changing my mind again; if she wanted me to pretend to be my uncle, that was all right by me. The desperate wildness of the escapade, the near certainty of being found out, this was now its main attraction.

106

Near certainty was wrong. Why deceive ourselves? The moment the cousins clapped eyes on us they knew we were not man and wife. Our desperation became gay as we realised it. Nadia was more excited than desperate, to be accurate. She would live by no rules she had not made herself. That was the attitude she conveyed, and who could do that but a goddess? It was not Nadia but Nut's face that floated against the sky.

In spite of her apotheosis and my capitulation Nadia still pretended to be angry. She shouted at the gharry driver, who was gawping at us from a distance of a dozen yards or so, to take himself off, get back up on to his seat and mind his own business. She swung her hat in a semi-circle to indicate the expanse of the Nile now puckering here and there as the breezes caught and, beyond, the low, pink hills smoking in the distance. "These are the earliest things I remember. I was pushed along in a little carriage to look at the boats."

"It's beautiful."

"No, it's very boring," she said.

"Don't talk for effect." Her aura was supernatural but it didn't quite rob me of my critical faculties.

"Listen! You will always remember me."

"Don't talk like that. Nadia, we'll live here, if that's what you want. I don't know what you mean, saying it's boring. It's beautiful."

Truthfully, I saw her transformed and felt myself transformed. She seemed to love me, but at the same time to laugh at me. "You're so –" She pursed her lips and shook her head. "You're more like a woman than a man. I mean, a girl. Like I was, when I was twelve. You make love, but just as though you didn't know what for."

"You're changing me. I feel I can do anything."

"I've always felt I could do anything."

I told her about the Goddess Nut in the Cairo Museum, said she *was* the Goddess and that she made me feel not quite human too.

"You're so touchingly innocent," she said, in her Eng.Lit. manner, "and that's why you do me good."

By the time we got back to town it was dark and the mosquitoes were biting. At the house of Nadia's cousins a servant went over us with a flit gun before we were allowed to pass the gauze curtains that hung in the hall. The house smelt strongly of incense which Mari said she was burning to deter the mosquitoes. They were a new sort brought in accidentally by aircraft from West Africa. Virulent malaria of a kind they had not seen before was killing a lot of people. In the bedroom the mosquitoes danced round the naked electric light bulb and Yusif, who had followed us up, clapped his hands as though to frighten them away. The double bed was draped with netting, and it looked as though there might be somebody dead in there.

The bedroom gave on to a garden where, by the light coming from a room below, ripe loofahs could be seen hanging from a trellis. Perhaps that room down there was the kitchen. The night smells were not of the dusty garden but of burning fat. We were both hungry, but we didn't want to go downstairs and join Mari and Yusif and all the others – it was going to be quite a party judging by the number of voices we could hear – though I guessed that Uncle Raymond would have gone down and met everyone if he'd been there. It seemed natural to speculate what he would be doing if he were there and I was not.

"It's like a dream," I told Nadia.

"You can't make up real dreams. They just come to you. We've made this one up and it could be changed."

But I had the disturbing idea that the room, the mosquitoes, the smell of burning fat and Nadia, coming in from the verandah, with a wary, questioning expression on her face, and I in a sweat of lust for her, were all being dreamed by Uncle Raymond, hundreds of miles away in his Canal Zone tent. Certainly he felt close. The kith and kin game, I have thought since, is sometimes played differently. There are societies where your mother's brother is nearer than your own father.

What was not foreseen was Nadia's brother Kamil coming over. He was a teacher in Assiut, about thirty, rather heavily built but with the same large eyes as his sister. His moustache made him look military and dashing which was not his real nature at all. He fluttered his hands and smiled all the time, even when giving the most dreadful news – a mannerism that could be put down to the inheritance of acquired characteristics: the conciliatory and placatory grinning of the generations of insecure Copts who ran the bureaucracy and collected taxes and sometimes became rich without being confident their Moslem masters would always put up with them. Anyway, Kamil was one of these smilers.

He came into the garden that evening where Nadia and I were waiting for supper, saying without looking at her but addressing himself directly to me, "I was looking for Professor Foulkes." Naked electric bulbs were hanging from the pergola and we could see each other quite clearly. He smiled and I thought this meant he considered the whole thing hilarious, which was not the case at all. To underline the joke – it seemed to me – he said, "As Nadia is plainly not going to introduce us let me tell you I am her brother. The situation is troublesome, scandalous and even dangerous." He nodded, showed his good teeth in a friendly way and said something about wanting to live quietly and without trouble. The mosquitoes were pinging about and I thought that if these were *anopheles gambiae* we were probably done for anyway.

"Go back home, Kamil." Nadia was speaking English for my benefit. "Give my love to Renée and the children and tell them I shall come and see them."

"I am not here by accident." Kamil too spoke English for my benefit. "I cannot go home until I have done what I was sent to do."

With this he produced a long, thin, newspaper-wrapped package from an inner pocket. He undid it and laid a British regulation issue eight-inch bayonet on the table, the point towards Nadia. It was quite clean. Not a spot of rust. It looked like a stage property in that muddling light. "I would have been here before." Kamil seated himself ponderously in the chair opposite and clapped his hands for a servant. "But I missed the train." Before the servant arrived and took the order for coffee Kamil covered the bayonet with a handkerchief and kept his hand on it, smiling all the time, like a galli-galli conjurer who would whip the handkerchief away and show us a couple of fluffy chicks. "I missed the train because of the funeral. There is much sickness in Assiut." It turned out it was his youngest daughter who had died. Hearing this, Nadia – who had stiffened up the moment her brother appeared – lifted her hands, cried out, rose and would have embraced him but he pushed her away, still grinning delightedly (at any moment the yellow chicks would be made to appear out of the back of my neck or the cup that was now brought him, on its tray, with its long-handled copper pot of coffee), saying in English that he cursed the day he was born and did not care now what brutal crime he committed, provided it showed how he could hate God and all the living. Why should they continue on this earth when Anastase was dead?

Kamil with his bayonet and talk of a dead daughter did not register in quite the way most people would suppose. Mr. Guirgis said everybody was much the same, irrespective of race, and this meant that Nadia and her brother were as English as I was beneath the skin. It was an easier line than Nadia's, that people were more different from one another than you think. So I couldn't be sure whether, by snatching up that bayonet, I should be saving Nadia's life and possibly my own; or whether I'd be making a fool of myself, and Nadia would laugh at me. I sat in my sweat trying to smack down the occasional mosquito. The garden smelled of insect-repellent ointment because both Nadia and I had rubbed it on our hands and faces before coming down. She wore white gloves. Her face shone with the grease.

Take sexual morality. If Mr. Guirgis had been Uncle Raymond he would have killed Aunt Treasure because a wife's loose behaviour disgraced not her but her husband; so he was entitled to punish her for it. Anyway, that is what Mr. Guirgis claimed. Women were not wicked in themselves (though they were certainly that) but mainly to the extent they brought shame on their menfolk: a husband, obviously, but also a father or a brother. They would have to punish an unfaithful woman if her husband – Uncle Raymond, for example – did not face up to his responsibilities and punish her himself. I'd heard of this line of thought, but assumed such violence was only to be found among poor peasants and not middle-class Christians like the Guirgis family.

Nadia was restless. "Anastase!" she said. After a while she announced, "I'm going to the church."

Mari said this was the wrong moment to go sight-seeing. Supper was waiting. But Nadia was insistent and went out into the streets where I followed and nobody else did. There was no lighting, except from the stars. We could make out buildings and the width of the street. There really was a church and Nadia led me into it by the hand, saying, "We must not let them separate us now, not even for a minute."

Except for the altar the church was quite dark, though a patch of sky with a few stars could be seen where there was a hole in the roof. Half a dozen paraffin lamps hung from the ceiling. At the holy end of the church a number of large semi-circular steps, seven perhaps, led up to the altar which was covered with a white cloth and a large golden cross that sparkled in the swinging light. The church was loud with the ticking of clocks. What looked like an English long case stood on the lowest step, on the far right, but there was a big, glass-fronted clock with a swinging brass pendulum on the left. There was also an ordinary alarm clock. Nadia explained the clocks were necessary for the ritual but she did not explain how.

Instead, she went and knelt in the semi-circle below the lowest step and, with a straight back, her wrists crossed over her thighs, she bowed her head, spoke first in Arabic, and then said, "I have made a mistake," as though there was somebody up there, at the top of the steps, who only understood English.

There was a stirring. I looked to the right and saw a goat, tethered to a ring in the wall and comfortable on what looked like a pad of straw. The sound of Nadia's voice had disturbed the chickens too. They were housed in a corner of the church and they began croaking, in a leathery way. The poor, dirty, broken-down church, was more a farm building than a place of worship. The animal smell, the stink of incense and the ticking of clocks, and Nadia praying – if that is what she was doing –

seemed to be saying something about eternity. I could not understand what the message was.

"If I can be forgiven and made clean," Nadia was saying, with her black eyes wide open and staring through the altar (I had moved in front of her to examine one of the clocks and now looked back), "If I am to be saved let it be through the innocence of this man."

Innocence, in my book, was still the same as ignorance but the way Nadia talked of it innocence sounded something you could acquire no matter how life-stained you were. So I didn't object at the time. Pure in heart – perhaps it was a notion like that she intended. Anyway, not ignorance or lack of experience. She'd been a good student and believed in knowing. If she'd been in Eve's place in the Garden of Eden she would have argued it was only through eating the fruit of the Tree of Knowledge real self-awareness could come, and without self-awareness there was no virtue. As one of the angels – Nut was an angel, no less – she would have had to argue against any fruit being forbidden; she would want a more positive kind of innocence, one you could choose, or it might be chosen for you. "God might choose to make you so," she said at one point in our talk, after I'd said I wasn't as innocent as she made out. Even now I do not know for sure whether she was saying anything of great significance or just disinfecting the past.

"At least Anastase is saved," she whispered through the ticking of the clocks.

"You're fine. There's nothing the matter with you. You've got nothing to be sorry about."

"You say what I want to hear. Cozens, say it again! It's a bit like absolution, what you just said. But it's not enough. Nothing will ever be enough. Nothing." We watched the goat chewing and the way its little beard bobbed under the mobile white chin, as it seemingly considered Nadia's outburst; but the animal was coming to no apparent conclusion and in any case we could not wait.

Back at the house we went straight up to the bedroom and, in spite of pleas from Mari, would not go down and join the

112

rest of the family for supper. Nadia said she felt too ill. A servant brought up food on a tray: sweet potatoes, thick bean soup, meat balls, bread and white cheese. We sat on the floor to eat it, listening to the talk going on downstairs. Occasionally Nadia went to the door to hear better.

"I have destroyed myself, and I have destroyed you too." Nadia was calm, even cheerful. "It was unnecessary. I didn't know there'd be you to redeem me."

This wasn't my view of myself at the time but it didn't seem worth arguing about. She was my goddess. I looked at the world through her eyes; I resented Uncle Raymond as she did, even saw a certain mad justification for doing the dirt on him by vindictive fornication. Redeem! Possibly the word meant something different to her. To me it meant changed, made better, saved; I couldn't see what kind of saving I could be responsible for.

We went to bed and made love under the mosquito netting. We lay there, listening to the talk that was still going on down below, not clear enough to make out the words even if I could have understood them. Above that rumble we could hear the beating of our hearts and the whine of mosquitoes.

"I'm sorry," she said, touching my face with her hand, because she guessed I was crying. She rubbed her hand in my tears and smeared them across my face, across my mouth, and I tasted how salt they were.

She actually laughed. "We've made a great drama for ourselves."

We kissed. She had hiccups and I kissed her as she hiccupped. She giggled when she could manage it. "*Special* kisses," she said, as though we had discovered a new and delicious perversion. Her mouth on mine and tongues quivering, she would hold herself in silence and then suddenly and helplessly hiccup and giggle so that I could feel her whole body leap and I could taste the sweetness of her through her breath. Everything Nadia did was right. Even when she said the only way really to hurt a man was in his sexual pride, by making him a cuckold and a laughing stock and then taking him to bed, like Uncle Raymond, and finding the battle had been won because he couldn't do it any more, she had castrated him. He was impotent, he was broken down, he was finally humiliated and defeated. It was her turn to cry then, saying she had been wicked, that God, even through the mediation of the Virgin, would not save her; and why had I, she said, comically angry, been so slow in coming? Why had I been late? Why had God not presented me to her the moment she knew Uncle Raymond was already married? "I want him to forgive me too," she said in a surprisingly matter-of-fact way. "Now that I have become so happy.

"Late! Late! Late! Like for the train at Cairo station."

She woke me. It was so dark even the position of the window could not be made out through the mosquito netting.

"There's someone at the door."

It was locked. I had heard nothing. I lifted the netting and climbed out of the bed, grabbing my pyjama trousers from a chair and putting them on in the darkness before going to the light switch. The door must have been one of those Yusif had in mind when he spoke of the detail of these houses being slipshod. It burst open, the lock ripped from the woodwork, as the light came on and there was a man I had not seen before, a professional thug by the look of him, with a creased unshaven face, and wearing a striped black and yellow brocade waistcoat. Nadia's screams were extraordinarily loud and high pitched. Behind the man in the black and yellow waistcoat was Kamil, looking really quite peculiar, embarrassed and frenzied at the same time. Nadia's screaming momentarily froze everybody. It was animal, pig-like screaming of a kind I'd not heard since grandfather did his killing and the pig was hauled up on a rope to have its throat cut, jetting blood, so bright, so scarlet on the snow it had always stood for my understanding of how sins could be washed away by blood, washed clean and white in the blood of the Lamb.

"Cozens, they kill us!" She never called me by anything but my surname and this last cry sounded just that little bit more authoritative because of it. The affirmation came from the heights. She raised her hands and welcomed me to the skies.

What felled me I don't know. When I was being sewn up in

114

hospital they said it must have been some heavy object, wood rather than metal because the bone would have fractured differently under metal. One theory was the blows were struck – there were four according to the M.O. – one flat across the bridge of the nose, one across the right cheek-bone, one under the left ear and one across the back of the head, though that gash could have been caused by my head striking the ground. It was probably done with the wooden stock of a shotgun, though I couldn't see how such a weapon could be swung in that confined space; and to have a shotgun as well as the bayonet would indicate an uncertainty about the way the murder was to be carried out. I used to have arguments about this. One suggestion was that the gun was never thought of except as an improvised club to knock me cold. They didn't want all the fuss that would follow the murder of a British soldier. So, put me out of the way and go for Nadia with the bayonet.

The evidence given at the court martial revealed I was found in an irrigation ditch soon after dawn by a peasant who draped me over a donkey and took me into town. I remember lying on a boarded floor while my face and torso were washed by an old woman who kept dipping her cloth in a zinc bucket. My pyjama trousers were back to front; so much for dressing in the dark!

Behind the woman stood Mr. Guirgis wearing a tarboosh with the black tassel in front. This was the one and only occasion I saw him so dressed and I tried to remember what I'd been told about the significance of the tassel. Normally it was worn at the back; if worn at the front it indicated strong feeling of some sort – rage or pugnacity. His pretence that Nadia had been joking with me had been punctured. The telephone line to Yusif in Assiut must have been red hot. So far as I was concerned it was Mr. Guirgis's last metamorphosis, this time into a fighting bantam cock. Anyway, I was right. He'd been on that train. He had spread his diabolical wings in the storm and was now a spitting miniature with scarlet wattles. At his side was a red-capped corporal of the Military Police with a revolver strapped to his hip like a cowboy. The British Army had no regular business in that town so I supposed he had come for me.

"Where's Nadia?" I managed to push the words in Mr. Guirgis's direction but he just shook his wattles at me and that was quite enough to make me pass out again.

Uncle Raymond came to see me in hospital. It was the Scottish in Dokki where they specialised in head injuries, for the first theory was that I had brain damage and it was this that prevented me from talking.

My broken nose and splintered cheek-bone were not sufficient explanation for the muteness. Interest centred on a slight depression at the right side of the skull. I had some broken ribs and a punctured lung but that wasn't taken seriously. The Army was mad keen to get me well enough to face a court martial. The fact remained, I was totally incapable of uttering a word. I sweated at it but all I could manage was a grunt or two. My chest was strapped up, I had a bandage round my temples as in the conventional picture of a wounded soldier and a special sort of neck rest to take the weight off the back of my head.

"You are lucky." Uncle Raymond sat at my bedside and spoke with exaggerated stiffness, like a drunk intent on clear articulation. "You have suffered some physical punishment. What mental punishment I can only guess at. Perhaps, on account of that, you feel no remorse. You may think you have paid your debts. But not to me. Perhaps the idea of a crime for which you are truly responsible is beyond your understanding."

He looked about seventy. The more he talked the more his mouth wobbled. It was an odd reversal of roles. Not so long ago he was in hospital and I was visiting him. That was when he had first told me about Nadia and I'd thought she was some middle-aged, dark woman. Now she was dead and I did not even know where she was buried.

"You're young," Uncle Raymond went on, "and if you recover, as you will, and if you survive this war, as you will, and if we win it, as we shall, all your life will be in front of you. Some day you will marry. I wouldn't tell your wife about this business, if I were you. Keep it dark. Women don't understand this sort of thing."

116

He never learned. So far as he could see he had made two bad marriages, that's all. Confidentiality was still his watchword. Keep it mum! Don't split! Preserve the conventions!

"I realise now," he went on, "that I should never have married. I am not endowed for it. What *seems* and what *is*. It's hard to learn the lesson that there's a difference between the two, though as I used to tell my students it is the central message of English literature. I've been a poor follower of my own discipline. Perhaps I should have studied something else. I've always fancied geology. It has nothing to do with human beings, and you're dealing with things that are very, very old. Perspective, that's what I've yearned for. Theology might have done. Now, if I'd studied geology or theology I would never have met Nadia, your aunt, that is." He still wanted me to know exactly where I stood. "What can we say of her now, you and I as man to man? Well, she must have had a most unusual hormone flow, and that's a fact."

In spite of what the bloody old fraud said about not marrying it was clear he still believed he could have made a success of it with the right woman. What sort of woman? Well, flat-chested. Serious. Interested in gardening, fell walking, *The Times* crossword. Whereas Aunt Treasure must have been a bit of a girl in her way, though not in the same league as Nadia.

"The hormone flow," he insisted, "must have been copious. I wrongly acted on the assumption she was like anyone else. What does that mean, 'like anyone else'? She was Egyptian. I ought to have remembered St. Antony. Always been something *odd* about Egyptian women. St. Antony thought so. It influenced his thinking. Do you suppose deep down he too was just terribly disappointed with himself and sort of inadequate? Couldn't cope, so he rationalised his defeat and went into the desert. I've always been a fighter, though. I don't accept defeat. There's a moral in this somewhere if only you knew where to look for it."

He had taken to picking his nose as an aid to thought. A Coptic funeral is a grand affair involving black horses, an enormous glass-sided hearse bedecked with jet plumes and women in veils wailing behind shutters. Uncle Raymond described one in

117

detail. I had feared that a woman who met her end as Nadia had wouldn't merit a funeral at all and had been tormented by the thought they might have thrown her in the Nile. It was a relief to hear about the funeral. But she was a goddess and whatever happened to her body she would be serene in the heavens. Day after day, and the interminable nights, were consumed in fury that they had let *me* live.

Uncle Raymond continued. "When I was young I wanted to be a writer but I'm not the imaginative sort. I could only write about personal experiences and I never had any really. The English don't, do they, any more? I sometimes think that. We would never have had this dreadful war if life in England had not been so bland. We'd have understood Hitler better. If I'd been German or French I might have been a writer. Or Egyptian, even. Nadia could have been a writer. She had this – sort of *rage*, you might describe it, never to be fooled by anybody. From your aunt's point of view –" he hesitated and with a curious delicacy corrected himself, "from Nadia's point of view that was too awful for words, being fooled. Odd! You and I might think it was happening to nice people all the time but Nadia wouldn't see it that way, it would hurt her where it hurt most, in her pride."

Is there no law in this country? Can you just murder somebody like that and get away with it? But at this stage I could not only not speak I couldn't even move my head from one side to the other or open and shut my mouth. They treated me like a paralytic, fed me with fluids through a pipe, administered bed pans, gave me the whole degrading treatment.

"I've been on a course – clearance of landmines," said Uncle Raymond as though to divert me. "I'm taking a unit into the blue. Absolutely the best thing. Just concentrates the mind. Sudden death, the possibility of it, just concentrates the mind. Puts everything in perspective. That's what I've always wanted, a real perspective."

With difficulty I could write. My limbs were affected too, but I could hold a pencil and scrawl big letters so I ought to have been able to write questions about Nadia. I didn't. I wanted to be told without asking. Where is she buried? Is it in Minia? One day I would visit the grave. But I couldn't put the question on paper.

On another occasion Uncle Raymond said, "Nadia led you on, I suppose. She's much the stronger character of the two of you, so there are times when I can believe you were almost as much a victim as I was. I'll tell you something, Tishy. I've come to the conclusion this is a very peculiar country. I don't know that I like it or even understand it any more. Such a mixture of pride on the one hand and degradation on the other." He looked around the ward to see if anyone was listening. "Nadia was an extreme case. But death is a great cleanser."

A special new sort of encephalograph showed I hadn't suffered brain damage so I was transferred to a psychiatric wing in Ismailia where Uncle Raymond visited me on the eve of his posting to the Western Desert to clear landmines in what turned out to be the build-up for the November offensive in Libya.

"Shall I tell you what I think?" he said. "One of the remarkable things about the human race is that it speaks so many languages. It's a very good thing. If everyone spoke the same language think of the inter-marriage there would be! A multiplicity of languages is the only way to keep miscegenation under control. Nadia's real life was in Arabic. I'm told it is a richly figurative language in which it is easy for the speaker to confuse some extravagance in words for the world as it actually is. Nadia was a very muddled girl. She had this excess of hormones, no doubt. But the language, her mother tongue, led her on, as she led you on."

Uncle Raymond never learned any Arabic; you couldn't waste years, he said, learning a complex language unless there was the reward of a great literature at the end of it. There was no great Arabic literature so he studied Italian and French and Spanish, or he would have done if he had the time, which he hadn't. "If only Nadia had been English. Speaking our matter-of-fact English speech, she would have been different."

It must have been difficult talking to a mute. I was pretty sure my face did not so much as register enough expression for

119

him to know whether his remarks had been heard and understood. The eyes moved but the lips didn't. He just addressed his remarks to that unsmiling mask. He read letters from home, but they didn't mean much to me. He'd had a bad time of it too so I don't suppose I should be too censorious.

Penhaligon told me later that Uncle Raymond had pulled wires to get himself sent up into the desert. He was, said Penhaligon, calm, bright-eyed, tight-lipped and religious. He actually insisted on confessing to Penhaligon which Penhaligon thought wasn't exactly proper because Penhaligon was not, apparently, that kind of priest. But he wanted to be helpful. Naturally Penhaligon did not tell me what Uncle Raymond had confessed but there was no doubt, said Penhaligon, he believed in a physical resurrection where he could give the dear departed a piece of his mind. If ever he'd been a theologian he would have been quite fanatical. His attitude to religion was not entirely healthy – not like his, Penhaligon implied, which meant taking it all with a pinch of salt. Broadly speaking Uncle Raymond had come round to the view the less people saw of each other the better, particularly if they hadn't been brought up in the same village.

When we came to say goodbye (and it really was goodbye because predictably he was blown up by a landmine) he knew I was being invalided to the U.K. He told me what a pleasant voyage it would be in the hospital ship.

"As for life," he said, "I regard it as no more than a desperate toe-hold on eternity." At the time this sounded like a quotation from some popular but meretricious mystic he'd been reading but I've never been able to track it down; so it was probably all his own idea.

He never told me that Nadia was still alive, but then he didn't actually tell me she was dead either, though his account of a Coptic funeral implied it.

chapteR 6

In the early 1960s I wrote *The Unintended Society* — it was published in 1964 and is now largely forgotten — prompted by Jack Kingdon, the psychiatrist, as one way of snapping out of the patches of acute depression that came up like a sea mist in those days. From the clinical point of view I'm so normal Kingdon said I illustrated the textbook. Take that hysteric dumbness. This cleared up on the hospital ship when I was able to convey to Major Brownjohn, known as the mad-doctor, I really did want to kill somebody and I ought to get out of the Medical Corps where the only people I could kill were our own sick and wounded. I communicated this information in writing. The idea of a court martial had been dropped by this time. Back in the U.K., then, instead of a discharge on medical grounds I was sent to Catterick for infantry training and ended up in Normandy on D plus ten days with the Duke of Cornwall's Light Infantry. It was all right. I talked. But I had no interest in sex. Kingdon said that my beating up in Minia was what was known as negative conditioning and if it had not put me off fornication for at least a while Behaviourist psychology would have suffered a set-back. It was remarkable it had put me off for twenty years. He thought it might have something to do with my acute depression, tried to introduce me to a few girls, but it was no good and as I was in the writing trade, journalism, he suggested I had a go at writing myself into a healthier frame of mind. He was right about that too. Hence the statement that I was normal. The truth remains, *The*

Unintended Society was written to stop me going round the bend.

There were misunderstandings about this book at the time. The argument, that well-intentioned social reforms and developments had unforeseen side-effects, led some people to suppose it put forward either a romantic reactionary argument or a hard-line Communist theory of the kind that said it was possible to determine the kind of society one lived in only by having the right kind of revolution. Not so. Unforeseen side-effects are the price one can reasonably pay for an open society but it was still worth pointing them out: the media are run by honourable, intelligent men and women but that didn't mean they didn't foster a change in the ordinary citizen's sense of reality. And without meaning to. For the first time in history values – ideas, that is, about what constitutes right and wrong – were taken not from religion but from entertainment: from novels, television, radio, magazines, and the press (because it was part of the thesis of the book that even the so-called hard "news" was part of the entertainment industry). The argument, that there had been a change in the ordinary citizen's sense of reality could only be put, it seemed to me, by comparing people in the Sixties with what I remembered of my own family in the Thirties.

The books that most influenced me were Riesman's *Lonely Crowd* and Hoggart's *Uses of Literacy*. From the first I took the idea that values were no longer handed down from one generation to another but created between people of the same age who shared certain interests and followed common pursuits – peers, that is. From Hoggart I learned that it was possible to write sociology autobiographically. So I said a great deal about my dad's farming, the undertaking business, Granny Foulkes's green-grocery shop and the like. Work was considered as part of self-justification, and Defoe was invoked as a Protestant exemplar. Tawney was plundered in a big way. I took it my family were living at the fag-end of a certain kind of culture where values were indeed handed down. The argument wasn't intellectually rigorous and what little success the book enjoyed had a lot to do, like Hoggart's, with the way it evoked a certain way of life that seemed to be passing away. There was quite a bit of publicity and one television interview.

After the interview I was having a drink with the producer in Television Centre when his secretary came in and said to me, "You're wanted on the telephone. It's a man who says he thinks he knows you. Funny name. Pen- something. Sounded American."

I went to the phone and it was Ronnie Penhaligon.

"I've just been watching the show. Are you Ray Foulkes's nephew?"

"Yes."

"I thought I recognised you. Well! I don't know what to say. I'm in London. This is Penhaligon. You'll remember me. It's a shock. What can I say? You really are Ray's nephew. I recognised you as soon as I saw you, and I remembered the name, Cozens. But we all thought you were dead."

It was less of a surprise than I might have supposed, talking to Penhaligon after twenty-odd years. I was still reeling from that TV interview. I was a fine one to be talking about the ordinary citizen's sense of reality when the bright lights and a scotch were enough to give me the feeling I had parted company with it. In a moment he'd start talking about Nadia whom he must have met, though never when I was present so far as I could remember.

"Who's 'we'?" I asked.

"Could I come and pick you up? It's just crazy, me chancing by in London and seeing you on this show. Hey, son! You're not dead! You know that?"

"I'm not dead. You can't pick me up here." I gave him my home address and telephone number and, because I was very tired by this time, suggested we gave it a miss for that night. But tomorrow.

"Nadia'll be pretty stunned, I guess," he said.

"What's that?" I asked, but he had hung up, and I realised I hadn't taken a note of his address or phone number. If he dropped me now I'd not know how to get in touch.

123

But he came round the following morning, clearly in a state of some excitement. It was as much as I could do to get him out of the hall into the one room in the flat where there were comfortable chairs, he was so busy talking. Several times he said he was amazed that I was alive. He was stopping off in London on the way to Geneva for a religious broadcasting conference – he was one of the American delegates to the Christian Broadcasting Union. His Middle East war experience stood him in good stead. It gave him an insight. The Union was busy setting up Christian broadcasting stations in the Sudan and he personally had fixed a contract with a Japanese firm to provide tens of thousands of radios at two dollars a time; one-station radios, fixed tuning, you couldn't get anything on it but this Christian broadcasting. And so on.

Still the same neat grey hair, still the same hardness, but he had shrunk a little and there were more lines on his face. He wore a check suit in different kinds of brown and white, a tie with what looked like a hand-painted spaniel on it, and white-sided shoes. The effect was theatrical. Any moment he'd start singing and dancing.

"What is it? Twenty-three years! Know what, in two years that would be a quarter of a century! But how come you're not dead? Ray's dead for sure and don't I know it! But he was real cut up about you. I remember that. You did *something*. What the hell was it? Gee! the arguments we used to have in those days – God! Right! Wrong! War objectives! The lot! I could see you were real committed, so I was sort of sorry when I heard you'd got yourself killed. Not in the war, though. Your Auntie Nadia was real sorry too."

"What d'you mean, Nadia? She's dead."

"Dead?"

"She was murdered."

"Nadia, murdered?"

"It was a family business."

"No, no, son. Mind you, I don't know what you mean by a family business. I was dealing with your uncle's effects in '42 –

it was the end of '41 he passed to the Larger Awareness, I re-collect – and I distinctly remember your auntie saying how sorry she was both of you were dead now. Not her and you. Ray and you. Not dead *now*. Then, that is. What's the matter, son? You all right?"

Just very cold and unable to speak. Dumb, in short.

After some time staring at each other, "She thought I was dead?"

"Say, it's just terrible you thinking your aunt was dead too. Not that you could have known her at all well but it sort of isn't nice thinking anybody's dead when they're not. And she, Sure as Sin, was clear you'd passed over." Penhaligon thought for a while, staring at me. "Tell you what, there must have been a misunderstanding, that's what there was!"

"Uncle Raymond went to her funeral."

"He told you that?"

"I was in hospital. He described the funeral."

Penhaligon looked concerned and uneasy, as though he'd been told more than he wanted to know; he hadn't the kind of mind that could grapple with the situation that had just blown up. Possibly I was nuts! Clearly, he couldn't think of any other ex-planation and probably wished he was in the Sudan dishing out those fixed-tuning radios. He was tired now. Behind the glitter had, all the time, been this tiredness. It wasn't fair, said those big dog-like eyes, that an encounter like this should have been sprung on him; seeing me on the TV screen he had acted on impulse. What was more natural than to contact an old friend. Now he regretted it. The kid had seemed crazy enough in Cairo, saying the Germans weren't as bad as they were painted, but now he might be a real case. What the hell! Everybody had grown older.

"My uncle wouldn't have said he'd been to the funeral if he hadn't." I was able to talk. The immediate shock was over and I felt warmer.

"No."

"I wouldn't have imagined a thing like that."

"You must have done, son."

"There was a funeral with black horses and black plumes on the carriage."

"Ray told you that?"

"He told me about a funeral. How the hell else would I have known? I've never seen a Coptic funeral."

"Yeah! But did he say it was your auntie's? There *was* no funeral. There couldn't have been."

"You're a bloody liar."

"It's no good losing your temper, son."

"Get out, d'you hear?" At moments of crisis one falls into cliché. And repetitiveness. "You obscene, lying bastard, coming here and – and – It's people like you with your black shrivelled hearts, going round and pissing on people! You won't piss on me!"

"You could ring her up on that phone if you wanted to."

"What?"

"Well, I mean if you don't believe me. Why should I tell you a story you can test for yourself? What Ray said or didn't say to you in hospital I don't know. I'd rather not pry into that one. But you've got to admit you were sick, I mean really sick. I'm sorry if I upset you, saying I thought you were dead. It's a shock to be spoken to in that way. That's something I'd concede. There's no ill will behind it. I don't know why you should sound off. Anybody'd think you aren't glad to be alive and your auntie too. She's a princess now."

"A princess?"

"That's why I'm in London. She's the one paying for these fixed-tuning sets. It's a real privilege to know such a pious lady, though I don't go along with the idea the Ethiopian Royal Family is descended from Solomon. That would make her kids Jewish. She is royal though. I honour that."

"Nadia's married?"

Penhaligon began hooting. "So you finally got round to believing me. Sure she's married. Anything wrong in that? She's the Princess Nadia all right. She's at Claridge's. You could phone her! Why don't you do just that? Then you'll see whether I'm a liar."

"Somebody is." After a pause for the information to sink in, "Or was."

"She's not only alive, son, she's got this ambition to convert the pagan tribes of the Southern Sudan. Did you know they were pagans? They're not even Moslems in those parts."

"But they killed her."

"Who?"

"Her father and brother."

"You've got to be crazy to say a thing like that."

"I thought that's what they'd done."

"Second thoughts, I think you'd better stay away. You'd only upset her. You've lived for twenty-three years thinking your auntie was dead, well it must have been painless, so why don't you go on thinking that way? You sort of shocked it all out of me. The Prince won't be too pleased I guess. Why should he want to meet his wife's first husband's nephew? Say, that sounds complicated. It's up to her. Put it this way. I'll mention it when I see her."

"Don't do that."

"You said you had to be evil in order to understand evil. Remember? I never forgot that. It was in Shepheard's Hotel and you were high with it. You don't mean you thought Nadia really was murdered by her father and brother? That's awful. It's not true. Why should they? You have to be perverted to dream up an incredible thing like that. If Nadia does agree to see you I wouldn't mention it. She just loved her family I'm sure and would be mortified to hear you saying such things about them. Even *thinking* such things. Say, this is an extraordinary coincidence! I wouldn't be in London at all if the Princess wasn't here and there was this financing of the Sudan project. Then I just happened to see you on that show. I'm very interested in coincidences. They show there's a Plan."

Uncle Raymond had lied to both of us, to Nadia as well as to me, or deliberately misled us. I had believed him because the screaming fitted in. I'd thought a lot over the years about Mr. Guirgis, Kamil, the bayonet and that screaming. What, I wondered, had Nadia thought back to? If the Princess really *was* Nadia. I was beginning to accept she might be.

Penhaligon must have tipped Nadia off. When I phoned Claridge's later I was put through to someone, a man, who said with a thick accent that the Princess was busy at the moment but would see me at four that afternoon if I came round. I didn't know who he was. Her husband, the Prince? He didn't seem too bothered whether I came or didn't, but perhaps that was simply the effect of the accent. There was time to go down to the office and do one or two routine jobs. They helped persuade me I was still in touch. Whatever I was being dosed with I couldn't deny it was reality.

Nadia, I discovered, had a suite of rooms, one of which she was using as an office; there were two secretaries, an English girl hired from an agency, and an Ethiopian, a young man with a blotchy face and a neat black beard. He was the one who spoke to me on the telephone. In addition there was an older man, an Italian, I gathered, who sat at a desk in the window checking figures. There were also, I learned, personal servants, a maid or two and a chauffeur. This room where I was waiting, the office, had quite a supply of those small Japanese radios Penhaligon had spoken about; there were three on that table where the accountant was working, some more on the main table and a pile of them in a corner. But there were piles, too, of what looked like tapestries. Along one wall was stretched a tapestry showing dozens of big-eyed Ethiopians riding asses, or walking under palm trees, or sitting on thrones, all in bright, simple colours, red, green and black. There was a big brass pestle and mortar of native workmanship. Saffron-coloured pots held what looked like sticks of sugar cane. Spilling out of a cardboard box were animal skins, long-haired and black and white in patches: white-tailed Colobus monkey skins. I was able to study all this while waiting for Nadia to come out· of her room where, the Ethiopian secretary told me, she was still resting.

Then a communication door, which I had not noticed before, opened and Nadia appeared, unquestionably the same Nadia, though a little shorter than I remembered her; and, of course, plumper. Her black hair was gathered up elaborately in one of those French coiffures that hadn't yet hit London. The eyes very black-lashed and heavy, a thickening of the flesh on either side of the mouth, white pearls in her ears, and the same long smooth throat with not a wound, not a scratch on it.

"We'll talk in here." I followed through the communicating door into a sitting-room with silver and red upholstered chairs and a settee. "They'll bring us some tea. That man Penhaligon phoned."

"He saw me on television."

"He explained that. You know what I now am? And who? He told you?"

"Yes."

"Ethiopia is not a rich country. We are only doing what we can to promote a little trade. Here in London there are a lot of people interested in folk art."

"You're selling folk art?"

We weren't really talking. She was sitting on one chair and I was sitting opposite. We were examining each other with incredulity. She'd been as shocked as I was, but by now I was beginning to get over it and grew angry.

"I swear to God I'd thought you died," she said suddenly. "I always wondered why the British didn't make more fuss. My father went about his business. My brother went back to Assiut. Nothing happened. If you'd been killed it would have been different. I ought to have realised."

"Uncle Raymond went to your funeral."

"Is that what he said? Yes, he would."

"You've done well. I suppose it's what you'd got in mind all the time. You said you had an offer from the Ethiopians. Is your husband with you?"

"He's in Addis." She ignored my tone and said, "You've shaved your moustache and your nose looks different. But you are really the same. Long hair, some of it grey, that's different

129

too." She even giggled and her eyes flashed in the light as she turned her head. This brightness of the eyes shocked in the belly like an electric current.

Tea was brought up by a waiter wearing white gloves. As he transferred the silver tray, the silver teapot, the china, the biscuits and the pastries to the table in front of Nadia she watched me; and when the waiter had gone, she said, "Think what you are saying."

"We've been lied to and tricked. At least, I've been lied to."

"Think what you are saying."

"It's a pity I didn't die."

"I might have said that once, about myself, but we've got to rejoice at every bit of life there is. I'm so happy to see you." There were real tears in her eyes.

"I used to think you were crazy, but in a way I understood. I didn't because I was too bloody ignorant. I ought to have known your father and brother wouldn't touch you. In a way it's your fault I didn't."

"Why is it my fault?"

"You made me believe that just anything was possible."

Nadia shrugged. "Everybody's got his own range of what he finds it possible to believe. Are you married?"

"No. What's more, I've lived like a monk."

"I have two sons and a daughter. They're back home at the farm."

We drank some tea and she said she'd thought I'd been put in a sack and dumped in the river. It was what usually happened. "You and I are privileged. We have had our own little resurrections in rehearsal for the greater Resurrection that is to come."

"You've gone religious."

"I live a life of piety and good works."

We both laughed at that, she had used her quoting Eng.Lit. voice, and when we had stopped laughing, I said, "I still love you, Nadia."

"Do you go to church?"

"No."

"Do you pray?" She swung into a lecture on the truth of the

Christian religion and how life would have been impossible for her without the knowledge of having been forgiven for her sins. "I know what you're thinking. Another old woman taken to religion and that's what religion's for, old women. That's not true. If you only knew me you would understand that. You never knew me. I didn't know myself. What a grace it would be, dear Cozens, if you too could know yourself and be saved."

"You're not old."

"It is my work to bring more souls to Christ. Would you like some more tea?" She spoke then at some length about the blacks who lived in the Southern Sudan and how tall they were as though this was something that needed treatment too, and how she was putting up the money for fixed-tuning radio sets so that they could listen to religious broadcasts in their own language. "It is real ecumenical Christianity in action. We Copts feel a special responsibility."

So what at Minia had reduced me to dumbness and impotence had switched her into good works and faith. No doubt it was what reconciled her to marriage with her Ethiopian prince; he'd be a Copt too. Knowing her dislike of Ethiopians I guessed she had the satisfaction of following her Christian vocation and mortifying the flesh at the same time. It had been indulged enough to qualify for lots of mortification.

No doubt she saw my bitterness and rage because she switched the talk to Uncle Raymond. "You know that when I found out about his first wife he just wanted to sit and talk about her? He had photographs, hanks of hair, letters, pieces of clothing even. He actually had some panties and stockings."

"That's just pathetic."

"It wasn't as if she was dead. He never loved anything in his life except that woman and his own stiff-necked pride."

"No, he loved you."

"You don't understand. He tried to make me handle these things! I sometimes wish I could actually meet this woman. I've still got these relics. I'd like to show them to her and rub her nose in them."

I was astonished by this. "You've still got them?"

"Yes. I couldn't get rid of anything Raymond left. After all, he was my husband."

"So you finally got round to admitting that."

"I was his next-of-kin. Tell me what happened after El Minia."

I tried to but it was extraordinary how little it all added up to. "I was ill. Then I killed a German. Now I work on a paper and I do a bit of writing extra." It occurred to me I was more like Uncle Raymond than I had supposed. I still had a few things that had once belonged to her.

"What things?" she asked when I told her.

"There's a handkerchief. And two drinking straws."

"Drinking straws?"

"You'd used them for drinking fruit juice."

"My father, he is dead too." She caught herself up in amazement. "But you are not dead!" She began to bubble with suppressed laughter. "You haven't changed much. You look thicker and hairier."

"You're thicker too." We both laughed.

But I was getting angrier. We had been defrauded. Uncle Raymond had lied, her father had lied, her brother had lied, all as a way of breaking the hinge on which my whole life turned which was the love that Nadia and I had for each other. No wonder Nadia had gone off to Ethiopia. How could she have stayed in the same country as the men who had murdered her lover? Pity for her, and for me, began bubbling up in such a way tears came to my eyes as they had come to Nadia's. I wasn't so much in control as I had thought. I was angry, then self-pitying and then – as though a switch had been suddenly thrown – wild with lust. In my imagination we were already naked and in bed again.

"And your nose is broken."

"Just flattened." I was what I hadn't been for years: male and ruttish. I got up and went to embrace her. Once more the great cliché. "I'm damned if I'm going to let anything separate us. We're married, we really are, Nadia. So far as real feeling makes a marriage. We're lovers! For God's sake! These years don't matter. We're lovers. We're one flesh. I don't care where the hell you've been. You've risen from the dead. It's spring. You can see the daffodils in the park. The trees are budding. It's the springtime. You've obsessed me. I used to think of you as a goddess who welcomed the dead. But that's wrong. You're Eurydice. You've come back from hell and blackness."

"Lovers?" said Nadia. She got up and went behind h r chair.

"You know what this is?"

"Not us." She actually looked concerned on my behalf.

"Don't you remember?"

"No," she said. "I don't remember. I couldn't possibly."

I saw how it was and walked out.

Penhaligon came round that evening to say that the Princess was worried about me. She was tickled to know I was alive but couldn't understand why I was so angry. It was almost as though I was sorry to learn she wasn't dead.

"Did she send you?"

Penhaligon looked uncomfortable. I suspected Nadia had sent him to bribe me. Keep quiet about our affair in Egypt and I'll give you ten thousand quid, that sort of thing. She was established as a Royal Christian lady, dispensing one-station radios for pagans, promoting Ethiopian trade interests, very rich – no doubt – and, for all I knew, in line to be Empress of Ethiopia. That was what her manner conveyed and she understandably didn't want to be rocked by an old scandal. No doubt Nadia's Minia cousins had been squared. And Yusif.

"No, she didn't actually, but she said you had delusions about the past and I feel a certain responsibility. Your Uncle Raymond was a fine man. He had a really lovely and lovable personality and I am under a great indebtedness to him. He was fond of you. That's good enough for me, even after all these years. Sure I'd like to help. We once prayed together. Shall we pray together again?"

"Balls! Uncle Raymond hated me and I hated him. He was nothing like me. He hated me because I slept with his wife."

"For God's sake! This is complete fantasy."

"Why should he lie about me? He said I was dead, didn't he?"

I had to hold on to evidence supplied, as this was, by Penhaligon himself; otherwise I might be tempted to believe I *had* imagined the whole violent, randy affair. And up-tight Uncle Raymond, had I imagined him too? What kind of wish-fulfilment was that?

"Tell the Princess," I said, "I want her round here at six tomorrow evening. I want to talk to her on my own territory. She needn't be afraid. I won't touch her. But she's got to be alone."

"She'll never come."

"Just tell her and see."

A story like this only gets written to make the past plausible. Nadia had one view of herself and I another. When she denied we had ever been lovers it was not simply lying; the truth was more complicated but mental hygiene demanded I accounted to myself for the life I had lived.

I don't know whether they read books in Ethiopia. There was always the chance some bastard might pick this one up and make trouble, so I went to a solicitor and explained there was a story I had to write but not publish if there was any chance it might hurt somebody. He said well why don't you bury it in the garden or burn it? You don't have to publish. It's up to you. No, I said, I couldn't take chances so (to humour me, I could see that) he drew up a document that was signed in the presence of witnesses. It became known as Cozens' Curse. It forbade publication of the manuscript unless Nadia's death had been proved. The solicitor said that if this was attached to the manuscript and it was lodged with, say, a bank, no publisher would touch it no matter how fascinating my literary executors thought it. Not unless Nadia was dead, that is. In this way the manuscript was protected even if I went under a bus the day after I'd finished it. The solicitor gave the impression he thought it highly theoretical. It wasn't every day clients wanted documents drawn up to prevent them doing dirt on their friends.

The story is put on paper to mitigate the sense of having been outrageously conned; by – what could you call it? Life? Except for Nadia and Penhaligon I knew nobody from that time. Mc-

Kellar was dead. So, apparently, was Mr. Guirgis. Razier I'd lost touch with. I saw somebody on a crowded Tube I recognised and he recognised me. We'd been in the Army together but even as we recognised each other our eyes signalled "Forget it!" If we had fought our way towards one another down that crowded carriage what would there have been to say? People haven't much to say to each other, not really, when they've nothing in common but a shared experience. It horrified me this might be a valid statement about Nadia and me, too.

Except for her there was only one witness to the story – myself, and I had to reassure myself the story was about Nadia and me and not, as I feared, about Nadia and Uncle Raymond, with me left out in the cold. Writing it down was a finding out. She'd actually kept Aunt Treasure's knickers. That must mean something.

I rang up Aunt Treasure (because I had actually made contact with the woman years before in the hope she might throw some light on Uncle Raymond's behaviour and, at least, confirm they were divorced; she lived in Leominster and ran a high-class tobacconist shop with a special line in pipes made from local briar root) and said: "You'll never believe this but Uncle Raymond's second wife has turned up in London and she's an Ethiopian princess!"

"Is that you, dear? We've got geraniums out in the garden. Isn't it early?"

"How's Tom?" I asked. Tom was her husband, the one-time Post Office engineer from the West Midlands.

"His leg plays up."

She was wary about this information I was giving her about Nadia. She was another who believed in leaving the dead to bury the dead. What's it got to do with me? she seemed to ask. An Ethiopian princess might have been a kind of rabbit for all she knew, the breeds had such fancy names these days.

"I just thought you'd like to know about Uncle Raymond's second wife."

"Yes, I'm glad to know, dear." She just wondered what I expected her to say about it. I could imagine her blue rinse glowing,

135

almost luminous in the half light she always lived in, "because of my poor eyes". Pink-rimmed, rat eyes. She was a fat, white rat in a blue wig that glowed out of an obscurity that was physical – I had seen her in it – but psychological too, because I had never taken the measure of Aunt Treasure. All I knew was that she and Uncle Raymond really had been divorced and that she had lived happily ever after. She was so happy she didn't give a sod for any Ethiopian princess. Why should she? She had a daughter married to a Labour M.P. and nothing else was of much concern.

"Aunt Treasure, what did you actually think of Uncle Raymond?"

There was a crackling silence while she thought. I could tell she didn't want to snub me. "Well, you know, he was all right, but I never knew what he was thinking."

"Didn't you *ever* love him?"

"Then he used to ask me difficult questions. Like, 'What are you thinking about, Treasure?' And the truth was I wasn't thinking about anything most of the time. He could never understand that. Yes, of course I loved him. I married him, didn't I? But he was a cold fish, if you know what I mean. I didn't know his second wife was an oriental princess." She began to shriek with laughter. "Well, whatever she expected I don't suppose she ever got it either."

"You mean he was impotent?"

"Oh no, not exactly," said Aunt Treasure after she had digested this shocking question. "Well, it's been lovely talking to you. In many ways you remind me of your uncle. You've a lot in common, I would say."

"I did an awful thing to him."

"I'm sure you didn't, dear. I know what your game is. You're trying to get me to say something like you've just said. I'm not sorry about anything that's happened, dear, that's straight. Morbid, if you ask me, dwelling on the past. There's enough trouble in the world without that, I say. Look on the bright side is what my Tom says, and I don't think that's bad advice. Lovely talking to you, but I must go." And she rang off.

Of course Nadia did not come. Even if Penhaligon had delivered the invitation, by no means sure, she probably wouldn't have come. How could she? What did eventually come was an invitation from the Ethiopian Embassy to a reception to meet the Princess Nadia.

It seemed a good idea to go wearing my old army kit, not the Operation Overlord battledress and tin hat but the Cairo off-duty bush shirt and tailored slacks Nadia used to see me about in. Should I remove the medal ribbons? No, time had, after all, passed. We couldn't turn a blind eye to victory. I wore the Guards' style flat cap, tropical weight, with near vertical peak, which necessitates having the chin well up to have any field of vision at all. In the long mirror I looked like the sort of man I had known as a recruit, a regular pushing fifty without a stripe, having seen fifteen years overseas service, in India, China, the West Indies (a favourite posting) who didn't get promoted even when war came, he was such a layabout. Come to think of it, I looked more like one of those elderly P.T. corporals with lined faces, hard muscles and flat stomachs who did lay preaching on the side. They had India General Service and Palestine ribbons, dark green and purple. Mine were dark blue and red and light blue; one buff with the central vertical red stripe, then the one with the white vertical stripes against the blue and red; and not forgetting the old War Medal 1939–45 with its stripes red, white and blue, with oak leaf. I touched them now in turn. Like one of those P.T. corporals I was fit enough. I ran in the park every morning.

At the reception this dated gear did not stand out as much as might have been supposed because there were a lot of Africans there in coloured robes, great shawls and caps, some with feathers and semi-precious stones in them. Laughing black clergymen in dog-collars and clerical kit were in roaring groups like rugger players before the start of a game. Board of Trade officials, BBC engineers, and the occasional Jap eyed me curiously. A little Indian in tight, white cotton pants asked me questions about different kinds of English beer.

Nadia was talking to some Chinese from the embassy in their

dark boiler suits. She caught sight of me, took in the tropical kit and medal ribbons, and her eyes flickered in a way I knew meant she was bothered by these signs of obvious psychological regression.

"Glad you could come, Cozens." She came over and seized my right hand between both of hers. She had acquired from somewhere a way of talking English that went with pink gin and long cigarette holders. Perhaps it was from her husband, the Prince whom I saw as an elderly Harrovian survival of the Twenties! "You'll have met the Ambassador on the way in. Did he tell you about facility flights?"

"No."

"You're a journalist. You could get a facility to Addis. I'd just love you to meet my husband."

"That'd be a bit risky, wouldn't it?"

"Risky? Why ever should it be risky? And why are you dressed like that?"

"I just thought I would. I like putting on the old uniform from time to time."

"Poor man! But you're not drinking anything." She captured a waiter for my benefit and then made off to talk to a bearded priest in a tall black hat who looked like Archbishop Makarios and possibly was. Nadia herself was wearing a long, dark green sparkling gown. Her hair was quite unnaturally blue-black. She had a tall white comb and a contrivance of pearls to control her bulky coiffure. At first I thought they were illuminated but the effect was simply the contrast of pure white against the black. No doubt her secretary had fixed this invitation for me and it could only have been on her instructions. I totally failed to embarrass her. She acknowledged the past had some kind of existence, but wasn't going to be inconvenienced by it.

The austerities, the two-roomed flat with its white walls and single ex-hospital iron bed; the long hikes in the rain along the Pennine way, a taste for military history (walking the field of Waterloo and checking where Mercer's troop stood and the squares of the Garde were destroyed), a view of politics that focused less on the people who made it than the extent to which

138

nineteenth-century Toryism and Liberalism and the non-conformist conscience were still operative in the 1960s (so that I had a bogus reputation, from the column I wrote, of being a journalist with a sense of history), all this had something to do with what happened in Minia.

Nadia was alive, that was the difference. Minia hadn't meant so much to her. Maybe her life wouldn't have turned out any differently even if she had not thought I was dead.

The Greek Orthodox priest had been joined by the Bishop of Zanzibar and a very tall, thin black man with an enormous nose, and they were all in one hell of an argument with Nadia who was quite plainly telling them all where they got off. The possibility of being alone with her did not exist. The Ambassador, with whom I now found myself in conversation, revealed she was leaving for New York the next day; so the talk in Claridge's was the only private conversation we were going to have, at least for the time being, and that was something she'd been shocked into. You couldn't say it was a considered act on her part, not a considered act like ignoring the invitation to come to my flat.

I touched my medal ribbons and helped myself to another whisky from a passing tray, in a state of such psychic overdrive I could have said, if Uncle Raymond himself had walked in – as I half expected – with his fly-swat and steel-rimmed Army issue spectacles, "Look, can't you see that we who were thought dead are all alive? We were lost and we've been found."

"She can't go to New York tomorrow," I wanted to say to this obviously short-sighted Ethiopian Ambassador who had hair in unexpected places on his face, in the middle of his cheeks and forked at the extremity of his chin. "We've got things to talk about."

"I hear you're leaving tomorrow," I said, when again Nadia and I were facing each other.

"Oh dear Cozens, I just want to go on saying you're alive. I'll have a bell made for you and ring it in a tower. And every time the clapper hits the bell it will say, 'Cozens is alive'. Why haven't you married? You ought to have children."

After a pause in which I heard this bell ringing in its Ethiopian tower I said, "I was married once. To you."

She turned her head and her eyes caught the light again in that belly-disturbing way. "I ought to have been prepared for the joy of seeing you, in this life or the next, by the optimism that is at the heart of the Christian faith. I certainly expected to see you in Heaven."

"Where there is no marrying or giving in marriage."

"As Keats said, a life of worth is a continual allegory. You see, I was a good student and I remember these things. I was a credit to your uncle. I've arrived at a dim understanding through Christ of my own allegory but I can see you're still working on yours."

"It's a star called Wormwood."

"What is Wormwood?" For all her reading she didn't know the Revelation of John in English, it wasn't on the university syllabus, and what Wormwood was in the language she'd read it in was not something I'd know.

"Wormwood itself is the plant that sprang up under the Serpent as it slid out of Paradise. It's bitter."

"We weren't in Paradise. Don't let us deceive ourselves."

"Something's bitter," I said, "and if it didn't spring up under that Serpent I've no other theory. It seemed Paradise to me."

"But not to Raymond."

So she could look at the scandal from his point of view! Something of the absurdity of two middle-aged people standing and talking in this way while a party went on around must have struck us. Or it may have been the single word "Raymond". We laughed. The black clergyman and the Board of Trade officials turned and looked at us because we were laughing so loudly. Nadia put out her left hand and I seized it, not knowing whether to raise it to my lips and then drop it, or whether to say, "Let's go, let's get out," and take her from the room. The scandal, dear Persephone! We laughed extravagantly and conspiratorially as we had laughed all those years ago after I had knocked Mr. Guirgis, her father, down on the dark staircase and we had seemed to say by that laughter that we too might be broken one day and others would laugh. They would be pitiless. But in spite of that we didn't want anybody else's love, or understanding, or mercy.

"He was just a liar."

"I put up a shrine for him. I must tell you that. You will have your Cozens bell and I'll pay a priest to ring it, but your uncle, I must tell you, deserved a shrine because he was so single-minded and good, and quite sweet, you know. I liked him very much, otherwise I'd never have married him. And he worshipped me. That was natural. He died in such a nasty way. I was told putting all the pieces together was quite difficult and they couldn't be absolutely sure they were the right pieces, if you see what I mean. I was upset and a shrine seemed absolutely it. Of course, it seems a bit pagan. It was dismantled when I married again. It would never have done for the Prince, that sort of thing. The bell will be all right. Do you know what, I think I ought to call you David now, not that awful surname Cozens which I never liked." She slipped over the word Cozens so that it sounded almost like Cozened.

All this time we were laughing in a muted, giggling sort of way, and it showed how on edge we were. So it was Uncle Raymond she really mourned. A shrine! What form did it take? Perhaps it was just a photograph with some flowers in front, though Nadia had spoken of dismantling it which indicated something more elaborate. Perhaps she had included Aunt Treasure's undies. It would not have been all that inappropriate. Uncle Raymond would have liked that. He would have said a shrine was entirely appropriate, it confirmed him in the status he had always secretly known he was entitled to, and from now on he could rest through all eternity in the knowledge that the past had really happened, some of it anyway (except the bit with Aunt Treasure in it) and was not an unshared dream.

"He was just an old man who took my life away," I said.

"I love you for that, David." Nadia, having observed me carefully, kissed me on the cheek watched by a putty-coloured man in an astrakhan hat. In a prissy sort of way she said, "But we can't always have things just as we want them to be, can we?"

It ought to have been dark, that time of a late spring evening, but patches of yellow and radiant blue puddled in the west beyond the budding trees. Overhead were wisps of pink cloud. I crossed the road near the Albert Hall and approached the Memorial. On the sunward side were weak flushings of light. I brought up under the group of statues representing Africa and, looking for Egypt against the sky, saw Orion. Because of the heat a lot of troops had slept on the deck in 1941 as the convoy slipped north. At nights we watched Orion through the Indian Ocean and I never see the constellation without thinking of those days.

From the Albert Hall drifted faint music. There were lights over there. Lights blurred across the evening from down towards Kensington High Street. It was cold in tropical kit and I set off briskly towards Knightsbridge where I'd take the Tube. Nobody took any notice of people's dress in London these days. By some standards mine was conventional. I kept my head up and hoped I'd be mistaken for a Guardsman.

Uncle Raymond could have prospered in some hierarchical and well-disciplined society, where the women had to be disciplined too. Perhaps the old Indian Army was like that. Or did I mean a society without women? I was forcing my mind in one direction and Nadia was drawing it in another. Sons! Why not mine? London had meaning only because Nadia was in it; no doubt there was a time when Uncle Raymond thought the same about Egypt.

So I passed by the Barracks and felt myself stiffening into Uncle Raymond-like attitudes, his walk, his cough and thoughts about Alexander the Great and St. Antony. Perhaps he was just an old fool who had done a lot of damage. Perhaps I'd become an old fool myself and only Nadia had the right attitude to the past which (except for the odd bell and shrine) was put it right behind you, the fall on the Pyramid, the outraged virtue, the towering pride, the love from a coltish Englishman, the lot! How else do you give up the wild life and become, as the Empress Theodora did in probably rather different circumstances, a Royal? (Though Nadia and she had *something* in common.) Looked at objectively, she was the one who had done all the damage, and yet she'd come well out of it. Perhaps she was in a trap and knew she could never escape. Her faith was the only way out. Pity it made her sound so smug. That was something you could never accuse Uncle Raymond or me of being. I had a certain fellow-feeling for him, in spite of that stuff about Coptic funerals, black horse-drawn hearses and the shining black horses which had trampled through my dreams.

By talking about Alexander and Antony I suppose he wasn't saying much more than that some are men of action and some are contemplatives. But this cuckolded, proud, dead man was wise enough to know you couldn't really choose. All you could do was try to escape from the role you'd been cast in. Just anything to get away from yourself; as I, walking in the cold air of that spring evening, did not now know how to do.